VAMPIRE AFFLICTION

THE VAMPIRES OF ATHENS, BOOK TWO

Eva Pohler

Copyright © 2015 by Eva Pohler.

Eva Pohler Books
20011 Park Ranch
San Antonio, Texas 78259
www.evapohler.com

Publisher's Note: This is a work of fiction. Names, characters, places, and incidents are a product of the author's imagination. Locales and public names are sometimes used for atmospheric purposes. Any resemblance to actual people, living or dead, or to businesses, companies, events, institutions, or locales is completely coincidental.

Book Layout ©2017 BookDesignTemplates.com

Book Cover Design by B Rose Designz

Vampire Affliction/ Eva Pohler. -- 1st ed.
Paperback ISBN: 978-1-958390-46-7

We have been trying to survive up here where the sun hurts and destroys us, where people hate us, and where gods punish us for things that we can't help.

—JENO

Contents

For my children.

First Drink

Jeno led Gertie across the dark night above Athens. Jeno's father flew close beside them, and a legion of vampires followed. Gertie was barely aware of them all, however. Her thirst for human blood dominated her conscious thought.

Trembling and on the edge of panic, she cried out, the sound of her voice foreign to her. It was more like a strange and desperate bird.

"What is it?" Jeno asked.

"Blood." She could think of nothing else to say. "Blood!"

Jeno's eyes widened with shock.

"She's been drained," Jeno's father said, in Greek. "She'll die if she doesn't feed."

They plummeted toward the cityscape and swerved between buildings before entering a balcony window and coming to an abrupt stop. Even though she was barely all there, Gertie recognized the cream-colored walls, gilded mirrors, and mahogany and maroon furnishings of the Hotel Frangelico.

The other surviving vampires soon joined them—Calandra, Jeno's sister, among them.

With cheeks full of tears, Calandra rushed forward and embraced her father. "I can't believe you are standing here before me."

Her father put his arms around his daughter and kissed the top of her curly black hair. "Neither can I."

They spoke in Greek, but, to Gertie, it may as well have been English. Despite her urgent need for blood and her feelings of disorientation from all that had just happened at the Angelis basement, Gertie was astounded by how easily she understood a language she'd been struggling with since arriving in Greece over four months ago.

The Angelis basement. Hector. The image of him running beneath her, from block to block, his bright blue eyes never leaving her as she flew with the vampires, made her sick. She hadn't meant to hurt him. She hadn't meant to hurt any of them. None of this was supposed to happen. She'd been a pawn, used by Jeno to save his father.

"Lord Vladimir," another vampire said, stepping forward with a bow.

Soon all of them showed Jeno's father their obedience and loyalty by calling him their lord and bowing before him. Some stood, while others hovered in the air, closer to the ceiling, to make room.

Jeno quickly took her in his arms. "I'm so sorry for what has happened to you. I never intended…"

"Jeno," his father called.

Gertie's throat felt tight, her lips were parched, and her stomach was burning, but she watched in silence as Jeno stepped forward, too. She could read his thoughts of love, joy, and incredulity. Jeno couldn't believe he had the opportunity to look upon his father's face once more.

"Father," he said.

Equal to his son in height, but with much longer hair, thicker brows, and an older face, his father embraced Jeno and kissed his cheek. Then he pointed to Gertie. "This girl must feed, or she will die. Bring me a human."

Gertie wanted blood, but the thought of drinking from another person terrified and repulsed her. As many times as she'd been bitten, she'd never experienced this overwhelming and nerve-rattling side effect. Trembling and near hysteria, she cried to Jeno, "What's happening to me? Why does he keep saying I'm going to die?"

Jeno reached for her hands and pulled her close to him. "I'm so sorry. I didn't realize how much of your blood I gave to my father."

"What are you saying?" she asked, afraid of the answer.

"You already know." He kissed her forehead. "I shouldn't have allowed myself to drink from you so frequently. My lust for your blood, and your lust for my power...But it doesn't matter. Now we can be together forever."

"Are you saying I'm a *vampire?*" she asked, faltering on her last word and feeling suddenly faint. Everyone in the room was watching her.

Jeno stroked her hair, the blond strands in stark contrast with his dark skin. "Not yet. First you must feed."

"What?" She couldn't breathe. The room was spinning. Her knees quivered and barely held her up. "I what?"

Jeno's father stepped closer to her with the enthusiastic boy she had met two nights ago in the elevator. She recalled how happily he had turned himself invisible and had reminded her of her own excitement over possessing the powers of the vampire.

"When a human is drained by one of us, it dies," Vladimir explained. "Unless it feeds on human blood. Then it turns." He moved the boy between them. "You must drink or perish."

The girl vampire to whom the boy "belonged" stood nearby and said, "Don't think. Just drink."

The same vampire had told Gertie when they had met not to think too hard and too deeply. Gertie remembered her exact words. The girl had said, "Life is what it is. Just enjoy it, dearie."

Calandra, who'd remained at her father's side during all of this, put an arm around Gertie. "The first time is the most difficult. You want to drink so badly, but you are also repulsed. After this, it will get easier. I promise. Just close your eyes."

Gertie hadn't expected such tenderness and compassion from someone who had attacked her the night Jeno had erased her memory.

Calandra lifted the human boy's wrist, pierced it with her own fangs, and then offered the bleeding limb to Gertie.

Gertie stared at the blood in horror, yet her mouth began to salivate and her stomach to growl. She closed her eyes and fought back tears. She'd never meant to become a vampire. How had this happened? Full of sadness, regret, and a terrible longing for the Angelis family and for Hector, she put her lips to the boy's wrist and drank.

"Turn me," the boy pleaded. "I want to be like you."

Gertie closed her eyes more tightly and gave into the desire to drink as she pressed her lips against his skin and sucked. After at least a dozen or more swallows of the warm, intoxicating liquid, she opened her eyes, refreshed. The room spun and danced for several minutes. She breathed in and out, feeling herself growing stronger. In all the stories she had read, the transformation from human to vampire was usually painful, as the mortal body died away and the immortal one took its place; but, she felt no pain. The warm blood moved through her veins, quenching and pleasing every cell in her body.

Something was happening to her bones, muscles, and skin. Gertie believed they were becoming denser, harder. Her nails, teeth, and hair grew maybe a quarter of an inch. In addition to the superior vision and hearing she'd already experienced while infected with the vampire virus, she felt her body become a hardened, invigorated machine. She felt spastic and caged and wanted oh so badly to leap from the building and into the dark night, to be free. But before she could run, Calandra and Jeno had their arms around her, and both kissed her.

"Thank you for saving our father," Calandra said. "We should all thank her, yes?" she said to the crowd of thirty or more vampires in the room. "Thank her and welcome her to our fold."

Each of them came to Gertie and kissed her on her cheek or hand, even though she hadn't saved Jeno's father willingly. They had used her.

Yet, she was moved by their gratitude, and she now realized they had used her out of desperation.

After they had all given Gertie their thanks and welcome, she stood in the center of the group beside Jeno and his family like royalty. The vampires looked to her in deference, because of her sacrifice, and probably, too, because Jeno was the son of their lord and they knew he loved her.

"What now, Lord Vladimir?" one of the vampires asked from across the room.

"My brothers and sisters," Vladimir said. "I have had centuries to think about what I would do in the event that I was awakened. First, I shall seek counsel with our Lord Dionysus. My hope is that he will agree we should attack the city of Athens—and other cities, if necessary—until the gods of Mount Olympus become willing to hear us."

No! Gertie thought, as shouts of approval rang out across the room. Everyone turned their eyes on her and frowned.

"She's new," Jeno said in her defense. "Give her time to adjust."

"We must no longer be treated as the scourge of the human race," Vladimir said to her. He turned to the others. "For too long, we have suffered. We must be set free to live lives of prosperity, joy, and peace."

Shouts and applause erupted in the room. Everyone there wore a smile, except Gertie, who wished she could disappear.

Jeno spoke to her telepathically. *Don't be afraid, and remember that your thoughts are an open book until you learn how to block them.* He squeezed her hand.

She got the message. She focused on how happy Jeno and Calandra were to be reunited with their father, for seeing Jeno's smile did bring her joy, even if everything else terrified her.

At that moment a dozen more vampires flocked in through the balcony window and hovered there, the leader pointing his finger at Vladimir in the center of the small, crowded room.

"Why should *he* lead us?" the vampire sneered. "He turned his back on us and has been locked away for over a millennium. What does *he* know of our suffering?"

Gertie glanced at Jeno, who squeezed her hand with reassurance.

Don't worry, he said in her mind. *I'll take care of you.*

"Believe me, I know of your suffering!" Vladimir said kindly. "Yes, it's true that I abhorred what I'd—what we'd—become. I turned away from blood and chose nothingness."

"Exactly!" the intruder said.

"But it was not nothingness I found as I lay there, day after day, year after year, century after century, listening to each and every one of your thoughts." Vladimir raised his open palms. "I know your suffering. I know it all too well."

"You were conscious?" a vampire from the crowd asked.

"Aware?" another asked.

"Yes," Vladimir turned to make eye contact with each one there. "For centuries I have been helpless to respond to your suffering. But no more."

The crowd hissed in surprise and shock.

The new group of vampires looked down at Jeno's father with uncertainty. The others in the room became deathly still and quiet.

"Why shouldn't Homer lead us?" the intruder shouted. "He's as old as you and has suffered and fought alongside us."

Jeno telepathically told Gertie that Homer was the leader of another clan, and that the vampires here belonged to his father's clan.

"Where is Homer?" Vladimir glanced around the room.

"Not here," another replied.

"I would gladly share his counsel, though perhaps he's best at telling stories," Vladimir said.

Laughter and snickering erupted, but Vladimir silenced them all. "That was no insult. Never underestimate the power of the storyteller." Then he added. "I'm not a tyrant. You have nothing to fear from me.

These people look to me to show them the way, but I would be glad to have Homer at my side. And it is Dionysus who shall lead us."

The newcomers seemed pacified by Vladimir's words.

"Dawn is about to break," Vladimir continued, raking his hand through his ancient hair. "Tonight, we should reconvene to discuss our strategies. We should meet in the caves near the temple of our lord. For now, invite everyone you know, then return to your hotel rooms or to your caves, pray to our Lord Dionysus, and be watchful. Stay in groups. Go nowhere alone. Report any suspicious activity directly to me."

The vampires filed out, like roaches in the Angelis apartment. Some left through the window and others through the door. Soon Gertie was alone in the room with Jeno and his sister and father.

It seemed their first concern was to make sure Gertie was okay, which both surprised and moved her, considering Vladimir had been trapped for centuries in a miserable state of consciousness. She was grateful, but what she really wanted was to be left alone so she could process what had happened to her. It hadn't sunk in. She could say it over and over in her mind—*I am a vampire*—but it didn't seem real, and, even though it had been an accident, she felt angry at Jeno.

Oops. She'd forgotten that they could hear her every thought.

"Your feelings are completely understandable," Vladimir said. "Why don't you lie down and rest?"

Gertie nodded.

"We'll talk outside." Vladimir beckoned his children to follow him to the balcony where the night sky was still untouched by pre-dawn light.

Jeno kissed Gertie's cheek and followed his father and sister outside.

Gertie lay down on one of the double beds and pulled the thick blankets up to her chin. She closed her eyes and thought that—just maybe—this had all been a bad dream. She would go to sleep and then, when she would awaken, she would find herself back home with the Angelis family. And she would be human.

CHAPTER TWO

Smoked Out

Gertie awoke, gagging and coughing. She opened her eyes to find herself surrounded by a veil of thick, black smoke. Her keen vampire vision cut through the veil, searching for Jeno and his sister and father, but no one was in the hotel room with her.

Then the door burst open, and flames leapt into the room. Behind the flames, Jeno emerged.

"Come on!" He grabbed hold of her hand.

Together they flew toward the balcony window, but as soon as sunlight touched her skin, Gertie shrieked with pain. Never had she experienced the feeling of burning alive. She screamed and retreated into the smoking hotel.

"I know it hurts," he said through gritted teeth, obviously suffering, too. "But we have no choice."

Gertie writhed beside him as he pulled her into the painful rays of the sun and through the sky toward the Parthenon, hitting every spot of shade they could manage along the way. When they finally flung themselves into the relief of the caves beneath the acropolis, Gertie dried her eyes and checked her skin, sure she'd been scorched; but there was no sign of damage from the sun.

"How am I still alive?" She caught her breath as her nerves and anxiety settled down. "Doesn't the sun destroy vampires?"

"We can endure small doses."

"What just happened back there?" she asked. "Is the hotel on fire?"

"Hector is looking for you."

The sound of his name had her head spinning.

Jeno frowned. "He doesn't yet know what you are."

Gertie flinched. She imagined how Hector would react when he learned the truth. Would he stop looking for her? She imagined Nikita and Mamá and Babá and Klaus and Phoebe and how horrified they would be. More tears flooded her eyes, but she batted them away. What good would crying about it do? She needed to be strong. She needed to accept what she was and move on.

"I'm a vampire," she said out loud.

She peered around the dark cave with her superior vision and was surprised by what she saw. The only other time she had entered had been that dreadful night Alexander had taken her by force, and, out of desperation, she'd come seeking Jeno. She had found him full of despair, weak, and starving for blood. As soon as she had arrived, he had swept her outside beneath the moonlight to protect her from the attacks of the other vampires, so she hadn't had an opportunity to look around.

Now they walked down a long corridor paved with uneven stones. Along the walls hung paintings of people and landscapes and cityscapes. She admired them in the darkness with her vampire vision, finding most of them beautifully done and quite old. Two other vampires stood talking but stopped and stared as she and Jeno passed. Other tunnels branched off of the main corridor, and Jeno led Gertie through one. It had a tapestry on one wall and a mural on the other. The tapestry was frayed at the edges and full of holes. The mural portrayed a golden ram—Dionysus—amidst dancing satyrs and Maenads. They passed a few more vampires along the way. One sat reading a book in the doorway of a chamber at the end of the mural. In a second chamber, another vampire was sewing fabric by hand. She looked up and arched a brow at Gertie as they went by.

Gertie wondered why all their rooms were open.

"We can see through doors," Jeno said in reply to her thoughts. "We get better airflow throughout the caves without them."

Gertie and Jeno rounded another bend and passed a few more rooms full of vampires—some sleeping and others occupied in some activity, such as reading or knitting or painting. Two more vampires flew quickly by them. Despite the paved floor beneath their feet, an earthy aroma dominated the air and reminded Gertie of the smell of a newly planted garden.

As they neared the end of the corridor, Gertie heard music. It sounded like a ukulele, which made her think of Hector.

"Not Hector on a ukulele," Jeno said. "Calandra on her citole."

"What's a citole?" Gertie asked.

"It's a very old stringed instrument."

Calandra's voice sounded softly through the cavern walls in a slow, melancholy ballad:

I agápi eínai prosoriní, prosoriní.

Kai eseís, agápi mou, eínai prosoriní, prosoriní.

Merikés méres éfchomai, epísis, ítan prosoriní, prosoriní.

Sti synécheia, eseís kai egó tha boroúse na eínai gia pánta.

With vampire clarity, Gertie understood the words to mean:

Love is temporary, temporary.

And you, my love, are temporary, temporary.

Some days I wish I, too, were temporary, temporary.

Then you and I could be forever.

"Is she in love?" Gertie whispered to Jeno.

The music and singing abruptly stopped, and Calandra appeared around the corner with the wooden stringed instrument—a kind of square-looking banjo.

"I was…a long time ago." Calandra turned and walked away.

Gertie followed. "You have a pretty voice."

Calandra thanked her telepathically, adding, *You need to learn to block your thoughts. Your mind is an open book. You will hurt my brother if you cannot control your feelings.*

Jeno interrupted with, *Stay out of her head.*

Gertie gave him a quizzical look. "I wasn't…"

"That was meant for my sister. But she's right. I should teach you how to block your mind."

They rounded another bend and followed Calandra into a room full of all kinds of interesting things. Calandra was sitting on one of two feather mattresses; on the other was the pillow Gertie had given Jeno, and it was turned to the side with the embroidered words, "I'm thinking of you."

She glanced up at him. *You kept it?*

Of course.

Across from the two feather mattresses, there was a bookcase, a writing desk, and lots of instruments and paintings and things stacked against the walls. Lined along the top of the bookcase were three framed paintings. Gertie recognized Calandra and Jeno as small children in the two outer portraits. The one in the middle was of their parents. They looked happy and young. As Gertie moved to get a closer look, she could sense Jeno's longing for the life he might have had.

"That kind of longing does no good," Calandra said.

Jeno cocked his head to one side. "Like you can talk."

Gertie turned to study the other things in the room. Perched on the hutch of the writing desk was a collection of old clocks and a very old gramophone with a record mounted on the wheel.

"Yes, it works," Jeno said. "Would you like to hear it?"

He wound the crank and then set the needle on the record. Although the sound emanating from the machine was far from high quality, it was nevertheless amazing to Gertie that something so old could be so well preserved.

"Kind of like me?" Jeno teased.

Calandra laughed from where she sat, cross-legged on one of the feather mattresses. In the next moment, Jeno took the needle from the record, and his sister returned to strumming her citole, humming lightly.

"You and your sister share this room?" Gertie whispered to Jeno.

"Oh, we really need to help her learn to block her mind," Calandra said, making Gertie aware that her concerns about privacy had been overheard, loud and clear.

Jeno laughed. "It might be more amusing not to."

Gertie punched his arm but couldn't stop the smile from spreading across her face. She was glad for the distraction from all the conflict at odds inside of her. "So, what are all these gadgets lined up along the wall?"

"Those are Calandra's instruments," Jeno said.

"And Jeno's clocks," Calandra added.

The instruments were easy enough to recognize—they were made of wood in various shapes and sizes and had any number of strings—but the other objects didn't quite resemble clocks.

"Timekeepers," Jeno explained. "Very old."

"Jeno's obsessed," Calandra said.

"With clocks?" Gertie asked.

"With time," Calandra clarified. "You would think it wouldn't matter to an immortal, but it matters to Jeno."

"It should matter *more* to people with eternity spread out before them than to those whose life is but a brief candle," Jeno said.

Gertie wrinkled her brow. "As poetic as that sounds, I think I'm going to have to side with Calandra on this one."

"Tell her your analogy," Calandra prompted with a laugh.

"Analogy?" Gertie asked.

Jeno put his hands on his hips. "Okay. Suppose you're in a waiting room for five minutes. You could sit there and do nothing or read a few pages of a book or listen to music—it wouldn't matter. Five minutes isn't much time to endure, right?"

"I'm with you so far," Gertie said.

"Now, imagine you must wait in that same room for an entire week, or a month, or a year. You could just sit there, but the minutes would seem to drag at an intolerably slow pace, and you might even go mad with boredom; but, if you divide the time up into shorter segments and assign an activity to each one, you will speed up time and enjoy the wait."

"Is that what you do with these clocks?" Gertie asked.

"Oh, yes," Calandra inserted. "He has a regular routine and doesn't like it when he's made to get off schedule."

"I like my schedule," Jeno said.

"It helps him to forget what he really is," Calandra said with a snort.

"Like that's easy to forget," Jeno chided.

"So, what's your schedule?" Gertie asked.

"I sleep each day from dawn until nine o'clock in the morning."

Gertie arched a brow. "Only a few hours?"

"That's all I need."

"You wake up automatically, without an alarm?" Gertie asked.

"I use the water clock, there, by my bed."

Gertie had believed the two bowls, with water dripping from the higher to the lower, to be a decorative fountain.

"The bottom reservoir is full at nine o'clock in the morning," Jeno explained. "Then the overflow drips on my head and awakens me. I pour the water back into the top basin each morning, and the process begins again."

"Don't you have to eventually add more water?" Gertie asked.

"Yes. Every so often. I try to keep the top basin full."

"Okay. Then what?" Gertie crossed her arms.

He took a pocket watch from the top of the writing desk. "Then I wind up this pocket watch."

"A pocket watch?" Gertie giggled. "But you have no pockets!" She was still adjusting to her x-ray vision and to the knowledge that Jeno—

and most of the vampires—never wore real clothes. He created the illusion of clothes. Where would he keep a pocket watch?

"Touche." Jeno smiled wide.

So glad you find my thoughts entertaining, she said in his head.

"For your information, I wear the chain around my neck." He put it on to demonstrate.

Sexy. The watch hung down to his abs, just above his belly button.

"Oh, please!" Calandra said. "Get back to describing your schedule!"

"Sorry." Gertie managed to blush.

"I take this pocket watch down to the Underworld where I serve Lord Hades."

Gertie's eyes widened. "Lord Hades? You never mentioned you know Hades. Oh my gosh, how exciting! Will you introduce me to him?"

"I rarely see him, and I don't know if I could arrange for you to meet him, but you could come with me, and perhaps by chance…"

"What do you do in the Underworld?"

"I take care of his horses. Before my mother took our lives, that's what we did. We had a farm, and Calandra and I took care of our horses."

"Do you go with him, then?" Gertie asked Jeno's sister.

"I used to," Calandra said. "For centuries, we went together. I probably will again. I just have other interests now."

"She's very good at writing songs," Jeno explained. "And she performs them at some of the local bars."

"I didn't know that. For mortals, too?"

"For everyone," she said. "For anyone who will listen."

"She's very talented."

"Oh, stop."

Gertie smiled at the siblings. It was obvious they cared for one another. It made her miss Nikita and Klaus, and even Phoebe.

"When my pocket watch stops ticking," Jeno continued, "I know it's time to come back. It lasts three hours. So I always return around noon."

"And then it's bath time," Calandra said.

"What?" Gertie laughed, trying to imagine it. "Don't tell me you have a bathtub down here."

Jeno smiled. "I bathe in the pool down the hall."

"You have a pool?"

"A natural spring—the last of what remains of Poseidon's gift to this city—feeds into a large basin. That's where I get the water for this clepsydra." He pointed to the water clock. "I'll show it to you later."

"He bathes for exactly a half hour," Calandra teased. "No matter how dirty he gets with Hades's horses, it's always the same."

"How do you know when a half hour is up?" Gertie asked.

"There's a sun dial in the cavern near the basin."

Gertie shuddered, recalling the excruciating pain the sun had caused her moments ago.

Reading her thoughts, Jeno said, "Indirect light won't hurt you. A tiny crack in the ceiling of the cave allows a few rays to shine down on my sun dial. You'll see. It's really quite breathtaking."

"Then what do you do? After you bathe?" Gertie asked.

"Then I read until dusk."

"The same books, over and over," Calandra said.

"So? I enjoy them. They are my little escape."

Gertie smiled. She felt the same way about books. She went to his bookcase and glanced over his collection. He had all the old Greek tragedies, most of the Shakespearean plays and sonnets, a book of fairy tales, and about two dozen novels, some of which she'd read.

"We seriously need to update your library," she said." And *Wuthering Heights* is way too sad for my tastes. I couldn't read it a second time."

"I don't know why I've read it as many times as I have," Jeno replied, "but I have loads more books in Patras. Maria, the woman I told you about, left me her library. I just haven't taken the time to transport it back here."

Gertie fingered some of the spines. "You have an impressive dystopian collection—*Brave New World*, *1984*, *The Handmaid's Tale*, *The Giver*…"

"Yes. I need to get the *Hunger Games* trilogy. Have you read it?"

"Oh my gosh! I loved it. You could read it on my e-reader if…" Then she realized it was back at Hector's house. Even if she ever got it back, how would she keep it charged? The thought of living an eternity without her e-reader and her huge collection of ebooks made her sad. "So, what do you do after your reading time is up?" Gertie asked.

"That's where my routine varies." He returned the pocket watch to the writing desk. "If Calandra has a gig, I go and listen. Sometimes I hang out at the bars. Or, I go and see a movie, if I have money."

"Why don't you use mind control to make the movie attendants let you in?" Gertie asked.

"I do that sometimes," Jeno said. "But it always makes me feel bad."

Calandra rolled her eyes. "I have never met another vampire with such a conscience as my brother. I go to free movies all the time. I'm not hurting anyone."

Gertie agreed with Calandra. What harm was there?

It's stealing, he said in their minds. *I'm taking money away from artists when I enjoy their work without paying.*

Gertie hadn't thought of that.

"Anyway," Jeno continued, "after a movie or a night at the bar, I will feed, and then fly around and enjoy myself for a few hours, if it isn't raining. Then I return here and go to sleep."

"He only goes off of his schedule when he's depressed." Calandra lightly strummed the citole. "Like after he first met you."

"Oh."

"Even when I lived with Maria, it was a similar routine," Jeno added. "I found an entrance to the Underworld in Patras, and so I kept up with the horses. And I sometimes came into Athens to listen to Calandra perform."

"And you don't get tired of your routine?" Gertie asked.

"No. Not usually. I enjoy what I do. I think the vampires who live from one moment to the next with no plan, like my sister, are more vulnerable to boredom and melancholy than I am."

"It's true," Calandra admitted.

"So what time is it?" Gertie asked. "What would you normally be doing now?"

Jeno glanced at the collection of clocks. "It looks like I would have one more hour with Swift and Sure."

"Huh?" Gertie furrowed her brows.

"The stallions belonging to Hades."

"Oh, right! Can we go? Will you take me to the Underworld?" She wondered if it would be possible to see her grandma.

He gave her his arm, so she took it. *We can go, but we will not see your grandma.*

"Goodbye, Calandra," Jeno said. "See you later tonight."

"See you," his sister replied.

Then together they flew further down the winding tunnels into a large cavern where light broke through the ceiling. It was the basin where Jeno bathed. Two vampires lay still as stones in the water with their heads lying on the rocky bank. One of them opened her eyes and looked curiously at Gertie before closing them again.

"We have to dive into the sinkhole to get to the Underworld," Jeno explained. "Ready?"

CHAPTER THREE

Warnings and Premonitions

Gertie took a deep breath and followed Jeno into the cold water of the cave and through a crack in the bottom. The crack led to three narrow tunnels that fingered out, even deeper, toward the earth's core. Jeno led her through one of them. Although she found it easy to hold her breath for a long stretch of time, Gertie was glad when the tunnel curved upward, and they emerged from another sinkhole in a different cave.

Before she had a moment to take in her new surroundings, a shrill screech made the wet hair on the back of her neck tingle and her heart stop altogether for several seconds.

"Don't worry." Jeno winked as he pulled her from the water.

They flew up toward the ceiling of the enormous cavern just as a dragon leapt toward them.

"She does this to me every time." Jeno laughed from their perch on the ceiling, out of the creature's reach. "Don't you, Hydra?"

"You might have warned me," Gertie said, catching her breath.

"What would have been the fun in that?" His dark eyes twinkled.

"I thought the Hydra was supposed to have nine heads. I'm glad the stories are wrong."

"She did have nine, but only *one* is immortal. See those eight necks at her waist?"

"I thought those were tentacles. Geez."

"No. The other eight heads were slayed by Heracles as part of his twelve labors."

"I thought it was *Hercules* who had twelve labors."

"Same man."

The Hydra shrieked again, spitting fire in their direction.

"She's not very friendly," Gertie pointed out.

"Oh, this is definitely her friendlier side. We wouldn't have made it past her if she didn't know me."

Gertie shuddered.

"Come on." Jeno took her hand and pulled her away from the cavern and through another tunnel, which was lined by a river of fire.

"We follow the Phlegethon all the way to where it crosses the Lethe River. See it?"

Gertie did see water up ahead. It was overlaid with a fine white mist. And all along the walls and ceiling of the cavern were sparkling jewels reflecting the light from the flames of the Phlegethon. It was actually quite beautiful.

"We turn here. That's Hades's garage. Mind you don't touch his chariot. He's very particular about that."

A figure appeared in the distance on the Lethe River—an old man on a raft with people standing behind him.

"Is that Charon?" she whispered.

"Yes. We aren't allowed to talk to him."

"Who's that with him?"

"Thanatos, the god of death. He's taking a soul to judgment."

Gertie could tell which was the god and which was the soul, because the former was beautiful and bright, with amazing blue eyes and dark, wavy hair. The latter was transparent and small—the soul of a child.

"Come on," Jeno said. "This way."

They passed the golden chariot with its black wrought iron finials and came upon a large stall filled with hay and two gigantic black horses with red, frightful eyes.

"Don't be afraid," Jeno said. "They only *look* scary."

He handed her a brush from one of the shelves.

She frowned, unable to believe such formidable creatures would allow her to brush them.

"They *love* to be groomed. They practically *purr*," Jeno said, taking his brush to one of the horses. "Isn't that right, boy?"

With a trembling hand, Gertie reached toward the other horse and then hesitated. "Which is which?"

"That's Swift," he said.

Carefully, Gertie applied the brush to Swift's lower neck. When the horse didn't attack her, Gertie brushed in longer, more confident strokes. Soon the motion became soothing for both her and the animal. She could sense his gratitude.

But Gertie barely had time to enjoy the experience when she sensed another presence in the room. She glanced at Jeno, who sensed it, too. Even the ears of the stallions moved.

"Who's there?" Jeno asked.

The image of a woman glimmered a few feet away, near the chariot. Gradually, she faded into view. Her blonde hair was the same shade as Gertie's but was coiled in ringlets around her face. Gertie blanched when she saw the curls weren't made of hair, but of snakes.

"Medusa?" Gertie whispered.

The apparition laughed, coming into full view. A falcon perched on her shoulder, glaring at Gertie with black eyes. "No. Megaera."

One of the Furies, Jeno said in Gertie's mind.

How are we supposed to act in front of a Fury? Gertie asked Jeno telepathically. *Do we drop to our knees?* Whatever it was, Gertie wanted to get it right. From what she'd read, the Furies were the avengers of the Underworld. They tormented evildoers in Tartarus.

"I've come with a warning from my father," the Fury said.

"Lord Hades?" Jeno asked. "What is it?"

"He has a special fondness for you, vampire," Megaera said. "You've served his stallions well for centuries. Out of appreciation, he wants you to be warned that this uprising will turn all of you into enemies of the Olympians. He wants you to know that if you carry out your plans to attack Athens, or any city, you will no longer be safe in his kingdom. You will no longer be safe anywhere."

"But we only want justice," Jeno said. "We want freedom."

"Hades would say that life isn't fair, but death is," the Fury said.

"And what of those who never die?" Jeno asked.

The Fury crossed her arms. "Consider yourself warned."

The figure vanished, leaving Gertie and Jeno alone with the horses.

"Should we get out of here?" Gertie asked, frightened for their safety.

"I can't believe this," Jeno said. "I've been coming for so long."

"Maybe we can talk your father out of the uprising. People are going to get hurt, maybe even die."

It's too late. Jeno put his arms around Sure and lay his cheek against the animal's neck. "Will you remember me?"

The animal, of course, did not reply. If it had, Gertie would have *really* freaked out.

Jeno next hugged the other stallion. "I hope to see you again, my friend."

"I'm sure of it." Gertie went up behind Jeno and wrapped her arms around his waist, leaning against his back in the same way he leaned against the horse.

They remained with the horses for a while longer, and then, as they were about to leave for the Hydra's sinkhole, a voice called to them from the flames of the Phlegethon just outside Hades's garage.

Thinking it might be Lord Hades himself, Gertie gasped and moved closer, with Jeno on her heels. But the image in the flames did not look like anything that would remotely resemble the lord of the Underworld. It was that of an old man with empty sockets and sagging breasts and a way of swaying back and forth. Gertie had heard of this person. It was the old blind seer, Tiresias—a prophet condemned to Tartarus for daring to tell the future, considered an act of pride and crime against the gods.

It was incredible to see him standing before her. It was like seeing a character from one of her books.

"Jeno Mimikopoulou," the blind seer said in a raspy voice. "Hurry back to your cave and save your sister."

Gertie's mouth dropped open. She turned to Jeno, whose eyes were wide with fear. He grabbed her hand, and together they flew toward the Hydra's hole.

<u>CHAPTER FOUR</u>

Death and Exile

Gertie and Jeno returned to the caverns beneath the acropolis to find them filled with smoke. It was like the Hotel Frangelico all over again. Vampires hissed and screamed as they fled the caves for the scorching daylight. Gertie followed Jeno to his room, where Calandra was stuffing her instruments into one of the feather mattresses she had emptied of its feathers. The white feathers lingered like flakes of snow in the black, creeping smoke.

"Oh, good! You're back!" she cried. "I can't get your clocks. Can you?"

Stones crumbled from the ceiling and fell about them like hail.

"Why is this happening?" Gertie yelled.

"I don't know, but we need to get out of here *now*!" Jeno hollered. "Leave everything and come on!"

"You'll be sorry not to have your things." Calandra stuffed two of his clocks in her feather mattress before following him and Gertie from the room.

More rocks tumbled down on them as they and other vampires scrambled from the caverns.

"The family portraits!" Calandra cried. "Take this. I'll be right back."

Calandra dropped the bulky mattress at their feet and vanished.

"Wait!" Jeno cried. "Calandra! Come on!"

Gertie's heart sank in her chest as the ceiling began crumbling at an impossible rate. She and Jeno charged through the rubble toward Calandra as they were hit hard by falling debris. Just as Gertie was about to give up and fly away toward safety, Calandra emerged from around the bend with the three framed portraits in her arms. Before she reached Jeno, however, a huge chunk of the ceiling above her collapsed and crushed her, and the searing sunlight broke through and scorched them all.

"Calandra!" Jeno rushed toward his sister and desperately dug through the debris as more fell on top of him.

Gertie was terrified that he, too, would be crushed.

"Jeno, please! We have to get out of here!" The pain from the direct light was unbearable—worse than the blows from the falling rock.

"I can't leave her! You go!"

Gertie rushed to his side and began digging, too, until a huge rock fell on top of her and knocked her out.

In another moment she woke up, feeling like she was on fire. She was being carried by Jeno away from the city of Athens in the scorching daylight. Beside her was the limp body of his sister. Jeno held them close to his body, trying to shield them as best he could from the sun. Gertie gritted her teeth and did her best not to cry out in agony.

"I'm so sorry, koureetsi mou."

In spite of her intense pain, she was able to read his mind. He was sending out a message to all of the others to seek refuge in the caves on his island.

"The island where Alexander…?" she couldn't finish her question.

"I'm sorry. I know of no other place."

Then something horrible happened: Calandra's body began to turn to dust and disintegrate before Gertie's eyes.

"No!" Jeno plunged down toward the island and shot down into a cave, landing against a crowd of other vampires, who had arrived before them.

The others helped lay out what remained of Calandra on the cool ground. As relieved as Gertie felt to be out of the tormenting sunlight, she was overcome with despair at the sight of Jeno's sister. Only half of Calandra's skull remained intact. Half had disintegrated and crumbled into dust. And only half of her body was left—the half that had been protected by Jeno's body from the sunlight.

"Why has this happened?" Gertie cried.

Jeno stared in disbelief at the ruined body of his sister. In another moment, Vladimir arrived. He looked at Gertie and read her mind.

"Who has done this?" Vladimir cried in a voice of desperation.

He fell to his knees beside his son and gazed at what was left of his daughter. Tears filled his eyes, and more fell from Jeno's cheeks.

Gertie heard Jeno's thought: *I've gained a father but have lost a sister.*

"This isn't fair! I've only just come back!" Vladimir cried. "After centuries of longing for you two." His voice cracked on his last words as he embraced his son.

How could this happen to her? Gertie thought. *Vampires can handle short spans of sunlight.*

"This happens when we're completely drained of blood," one of the other vampires replied to her thoughts. "The sunlight destroys us."

Other casualties began pouring into the caves in the arms of their weeping loved ones. Within a span of thirty minutes, more than ten crumbling corpses lined the cavern floor.

From the open thoughts of some of those still living, Gertie understood that there were more casualties that hadn't been saved.

"I should have left her there," Jeno muttered. "Maybe we could have revived her later tonight."

"Once the caves collapsed, the light broke through, anyway," someone said. "We had to take the chance."

Tears streamed from Gertie's eyes at the sight of Jeno and his father slumped over Calandra. Jeno had just lost everything that had ever been dear to him—his home, his clocks, his books, his only image of his mother, and, most importantly, his sister. Gertie had never felt sorrier for anyone in her life. Wrapping her arms around his waist from behind, she leaned her cheek against his back and cried.

I'm so sorry, Jeno. I'm so, so sorry.

There was only one thing Gertie knew for sure: if Hector had any role in this malicious act, then she wanted nothing to do with him ever again.

The vampires wept and mourned for the rest of the day in the refuge of the caves, their number increasing as other refugees from the acropolis found their way to Jeno's island. At night, they gathered on the beach beneath the cool moonlight to discuss where to go from here. Gertie was surprised by their number. At least a hundred were present. She was sorry for them and angry for what had happened, but she was also frightened for the people of Greece, especially for the Angelis family and for Hector.

Vladimir stood facing the crowd with his back to the sea and his feet in the shallow waves that gently lapped upon the sand. Two of the other clan leaders, who'd been introduced to Gertie as Homer and Euripides, stood on either side of him. They were both elderly in appearance and must have been nearly twice Vladimir's age when they were all created by the Maenads.

Vladimir cleared his throat. "My brothers and sisters, our first task should be to visit our old caves and see if any of those left behind might be rescued. It's doubtful, but not impossible, that there are survivors."

Homer stepped forward. "Those of you who lost inordinate amounts of blood during the collapse might first need to feed before all else." The old vampire turned to his two co-leaders. "I've forgotten what else I wanted to say."

"Reconvene here at midnight," Euripides said.

"Yes," Homer said. "Reconvene here at midnight."

"To pray in solidarity for the guidance of Dionysus," Euripides added.

"Yes, to pray," Homer said.

"When will we attack the city?" someone from the crowd asked, which stirred a lot of commotion on the beach.

Vladimir raised his hand for silence. "I promise we will have our revenge, but first we want to solicit the help of our lord."

"I agree," Homer said. "And I want to add that…" the old vampire left off, turning to his companions for help.

"That we'll be more successful with a god on our side," Euripides finished for him.

"Yes," Homer said. "Exactly."

"If anyone here tonight makes any move on his or her own against humanity," Vladimir said, "you'll only undermine our efforts as a group. We must cooperate and plan our actions strategically if we hope to enact change after so many centuries of subjugation."

"So be patient," Euripides said. "And reach out to other vampires in neighboring cities. Spread the word about what has happened and what we hope to do."

"But be discreet," Homer added. "We don't want the gods to get wind of this."

"Those who can go without blood should follow me to the acropolis," Vladimir said. "The rest can meet us there after you feed. But all should be on the lookout for signs of trouble."

"Back here at midnight," Euripides said.

"Let's go!" Homer cried, waving his arms in the air.

Vladimir took off in the dark night with at least half the crowd behind him. The other half went in other directions. Jeno lingered behind on the island with Gertie, probably because he had already read her mind.

She hadn't lost any blood in the collapse, but she was starving for it.

"It's because you're new," Jeno explained gently before kissing the top of her nose. "Let's go. I'll help you."

CHAPTER FIVE

Second Drink

Gertie breathed in the fresh air of the cool night as she and Jeno flew toward Athens. The sea raged beneath them, as though it sympathized with the vampires. As sorry as Gertie felt for them for their losses, she didn't share their desire to attack innocent mortals to draw the attention of the gods; however, she did share their desperate need for blood. Hers had become all-consuming.

The closer they got to the city, the more urgently she needed it.

As they neared Athens, her vampire eyes caught sight of the acropolis in ruins. All but the Parthenon had fallen into mounds of rock and rubble. The Erechtheion, the Propylaea, and the temple of Athena Nike were leveled to the ground. Gertie could only imagine how long it would take to attempt to rebuild replicas.

"It's been done before," Jeno said.

"The ruins have been demolished and rebuilt?"

"In ancient times."

"But that's different."

"Not to the immortals."

Gertie gave no reply but gnawed on her lower lip. Who could have caused such massive destruction to one of the world's most important monuments?

"This way," Jeno said. "Omonioa Square. It's where we'll find the willing."

They soared down closer to the city and landed in an alleyway between two tall buildings. Gertie sensed every mortal within a mile. She could hear their hearts and smell their blood. She cringed at her own eagerness.

"Don't worry," Jeno said. "I have a few regular suppliers who can help us."

She wondered how the other vampires did it. How did they feed from their fellow humans?

"Look, you can't think this way," Jeno said as he led her toward the square, which was really a semicircle. "You'll make yourself sick."

"I can't help how I feel."

"Most vampires begin to think of humans in the same way many humans think of animals—as nothing more than food."

"I will never be that kind of vampire."

He took her hand. "This way."

She followed him into a bar.

The smell of alcohol burned Gertie's nostrils, and the cigarette smoke bothered her eyes and lungs. As she and Jeno picked their way through the crowd toward the bartender, Gertie found it difficult to resist lunging for the necks and wrists of those they passed.

She was starving.

"Hey, Pablo," Jeno said to the bartender. "Have you seen Old Man Mikos?"

"He's gone. Already had his fill tonight."

"What about Aggie?"

The bartender shrugged. "Haven't seen her."

Jeno thanked the bartender and glanced around the smoky room. Then he took Gertie's hand and said, "Come on."

She stopped him and, feeling desperate, whispered, "Can't I use mind control?" She locked eyes on an old man she'd caught checking her out. He gave her the creeps and made her feel that, if she was going to have to stoop to treating humans like food, this would be the one to choose. "This one deserves to be taught a lesson."

Follow me into the alley, she said in the mind of the man, who stood up, mesmerized.

"Gertie, that's not the way," Jeno whispered in her ear. "Come with me."

Gertie broke eye contact with the man and left with Jeno. When she glanced back from the doorway, she saw he was still watching her.

"He wants to come with us," she said. "Why won't you let him?"

Jeno put an arm around her waist. "He doesn't know what you have in mind."

"So? He's a jerk." She followed Jeno out onto the sidewalk.

"For admiring you? Listen to me. You can't use your powers to punish human behavior."

"Why not?"

"It's not your place to judge and punish. You aren't a god."

"But…"

"Don't let your powers go to your head. That happens to a lot of our kind."

"Are you telling me I need to be a responsible vampire?" She laughed.

He looked hurt, and she was immediately sorry.

"Jeno, I…"

Before he could reply, he was thrown against the side of the building and held there at sword point by a tall dark figure in a hood.

Gertie rushed up behind the hooded man, attempting to pin his arms to his side, but his strength was equal to hers, even though she could smell his human blood. Without turning, he knocked the back of his head against her forehead. Gertie flinched and blinked and then lifted her feet from the ground and flew for his throat. Dodging the jab of his elbow with amazing dexterity and speed, she sank her fangs greedily into the side of his neck. The bite paralyzed him momentarily as she sucked and sucked the warm, sweet, and intoxicating liquid, making every cell in her body rejoice. After a half a dozen swallows, she knew she should probably stop, but it felt oh, so good.

"Enough," Jeno said. *Gertie, stop! You'll drain him!*

She opened her eyes and lifted her face. The dark hood of her victim dropped back from a blond head, and she gasped, as did he.

It was Hector.

He dropped his hold of Jeno and blinked against the spinning effect of the vampire virus. Without meaning to read his mind, she could sense his disorientation, dizziness, and euphoria in conflict with his shock.

Jeno pinned Hector's arms behind his back, and Hector didn't resist. Instead, he stared at her with his mouth wide open.

"Gertie? Have you…"

He couldn't bring himself to say it. The look of shock and revulsion on his face broke her heart. Suddenly she felt him in her mind, reading her thoughts.

She hadn't learned how to block them yet.

With wide, moist eyes, he gawked at her until he noticed the tears on her cheeks.

My poor, sweet, Gertie.

Before she could utter a word, Jeno moved between them and said, full of anger, "Tell me who was responsible for the destruction of our caves."

Hector had no ability to stop his thoughts. *Athena.*

The demigod caught Jeno by the throat and forced him against the side of the building once more. "How could you let this happen to Gertie?"

Gertie read Jeno's thoughts along with Hector. *It was never my intention. I only meant to save my father from the Angelis boy.*

"Klaus?" Hector asked.

"He planned to destroy my father along with his brother," Jeno said in a strangled voice.

"You know it's true," Gertie said. "Now please, let him go. He lost his sister today."

Hector took a step back and freed Jeno. "I'm sorry, man." Yet his thoughts revealed his true attitude: *But she was already dead.*

"Is that how you feel about me?" Gertie asked.

"You can still be saved."

"By killing my father," Jeno said. "Is that your plan?"

"I'll do whatever it takes to save her."

Jeno hissed and charged at Hector, who drew his sword and swung, nearly decapitating the vampire.

Gertie flew between them and held them off of one another, a hand flat against each of their chests, her elbows locked. To Hector, she shouted, "What if I don't want to be saved?" Yet, she couldn't hide her thoughts. She would like to be human again. She longed to rejoin the Angelis family. She hoped one day to walk again in sunshine and to no longer crave human blood. And she missed Hector—she missed him so much.

"I love Jeno," she insisted. And she could never hurt him. She could never take his father away from him, especially after what had happened to his sister.

Hector's face paled. Gertie wanted to cry again, but she fought back tears.

Jeno glared past Gertie at Hector. "Why would Athena destroy her own monument?"

"Athena never wanted your kind living beneath her temple in the first place," Hector said. "When she overheard your leaders making plans to attack her favorite city, what did you expect her to do? Sit back and watch? You tramps don't know what you're up against. You need to back off and be grateful for what you have."

"*Grateful?*" Jeno sneered. "You think we ought to be *grateful?*"

"You live leisurely lives with plenty of willing humans," Hector accused. "What more could you want? The gods don't begrudge you anything."

"How about status and respect?" Jeno practically spit. "You yourself refer to us as tramps. Others call us freaks and beggars. The gods should treat us equally with mortals, but they look at us with disdain. And we do nothing to deserve it."

"That's a lie," Hector said. "I've seen plenty of vampires take humans against their will and sometimes leave them for dead. Have you forgotten Alexander?"

Gertie screamed, "Enough!" She just couldn't take it anymore. "Go away, Hector! Leave us alone!"

"But Gertie, I…"

"Go away!" She narrowed her eyes at him viciously and wished him gone. She hated his attitude toward the vampires. It made her feel sick.

Hector just stood there, dumbfounded.

"Or better yet, we'll go," she said. "Come on, Jeno."

She took her fellow vampire's hand in hers and together they lifted up into the sky, leaving the heartbroken Hector behind.

CHAPTER SIX

The Winter Solstice

The next several days were short, and the nights were long as the winter solstice approached. During the day, the vampires kept to the crowded caves and either slept, prayed, or talked about their eagerness for war. Sometimes Homer told stories of the epic wars of ancient times. They speculated about when their Lord Dionysus would finally answer their prayers and lead them into battle. Some felt it was time to take matters into their own hands.

During the nights, Jeno and Gertie flew to Athens to feed, and then they went to the acropolis to pick through the rubble in search of his family portraits and other remnants of his past. One night, they recovered three of his books, completely intact, whereas a dozen others right next to them had been incinerated. They also found the feather mattress Calandra had filled with her instruments, even though the instruments had been crushed to bits. On the third night, they found one of the paintings—the one of Calandra as a little girl. This made Jeno very happy—and very sad.

After leaving the acropolis, Gertie and Jeno would spend a few hours back on the island. Sometimes they prayed with the others, whose numbers had doubled, and sometimes they went off on their own to stroll along the beach and gaze at the stars. Gertie rarely thought about what had happened there weeks ago with Alexander. She was determined to forget about the past and accept her future. When thoughts of Hector and the Angelis family crept into her mind, she pushed them away, refusing to dwell on them.

She could sense Jeno undergoing his own struggle to forget the past. Everywhere he looked reminded him of his sister, his life-long companion. Some days, he seemed to cling to the past, like when he gazed at his sister's portrait; and other days he blocked it out.

It was easiest to block the past while they were swimming. With their superhuman speed, they could move through the water faster than any other creature, and with their superhuman vision, they could see everything underwater for miles. Gertie used to be terrified to swim in the sea, but as a vampire, she had no fear of it. Jeno taught her how to swoop down deep near the ocean floor, build momentum, and then shoot yards into the air before looping back down again.

It still wasn't as magical as the night she had leapt into the ocean after Hector only to be rescued by his father, Hephaestus, in the form of a giant white crane.

Ouch.

Oh, Jeno. It was the presence of a god that made that night magical.

Of course, it was.

After that, he taught her how to block her thoughts from other vampires. It was too hurtful for him to be reminded of her feelings for Hector over and over again, and there was nothing she could say to defend or justify, because her mind was an open book.

Blocking the mind turned out to be a lot like making the body invisible. It was a defense mechanism, but instead of pulling all the energy inward, a vampire had to pull the energy toward the mind and erect it as a shield. Manipulating energy seemed to come naturally to Gertie, and Jeno made it easy for her to visualize it.

What didn't come naturally to her was going without clothes. Her one set of clothing was quickly becoming ragged and worn. She used illusions to make herself look more respectable when they entered the city at night to feed, because otherwise her appearance would only further reinforce the stereotype that vamps were tramps. She washed in the sea every day in her clothes, but that didn't stop them from becoming more and more threadbare as the days wore on. One night, out of desperation, she snuck into a department store and stole a fresh new set. Jeno was appalled but he soon forgave her.

Gertie also grew more independent over those next several days. Before, she'd been terrified to leave Jeno's side, but eventually she was able to make trips into Athens on her own. As a new vampire, she needed to feed almost twice as often as Jeno. Since it was familiar to her, she always went to Omonoia Square.

Once she was walking near the square when she came across the older women who had tried to lure her with their mesmerizing eyes the night she had gotten lost and Jeno had saved her. At that time, she hadn't the slightest idea that vampires were creatures of anything more than folklore and mythology. Tonight, the three older women were shocked to recognize her as a fellow vampire. A quick check of their minds revealed that they lived in slums in the city and were unaware of the uprising. Gertie wondered how many others existed in Athens who weren't already part of the growing army. These women cared only about getting by from day to day and shared no aspirations of freedom. They looked at Gertie with disdain. This was their turf, and they didn't like the idea of sharing the food supply with another.

Gertie hissed at them as she walked by, unwilling to take their brazen intimidation. She was as strong as they and had nothing to fear. They could kiss her you-know-what.

But before she had gone more than a few steps past the women, a group of six college kids—three girls and three boys—rounded the corner. Gertie knew they were students from the university by their school-themed shirts and by their thoughts. They stunk of alcohol and cigarettes, but the sweet smell of their blood was overpowering. One of them had skinned her knees, so that explained it. Gertie glanced back at the three vampires and was nearly overwhelmed by their bloodlust—both in their eyes and in the thoughts they didn't bother to guard.

All three vampires stepped between Gertie and the group of students.

"Elate mazi moy," the tallest and most beautiful of the three said eagerly. "Can I help you?"

"No, thank you," one of the boys replied with a red face. He thought he was being propositioned by a hooker.

"But your friend is bleeding," the tall vampire insisted.

"I'm fine," the girl said casually but then, locking eyes with the tall vampire, added, "Unless you can help me."

"We can help you." The oldest of the three vampires stepped forward, mesmerizing one of the boys. "We have an elixir."

"An elixir?" the boy repeated. He took a step toward the woman.

The first of the college boys to have spoken said, "Guys, she's fine."

The third vampire moved directly in front of that boy and said, "But what of your headache?" She locked eyes with him. "We can help you with that, too."

"Okay," the stupefied boy said.

An old man shouted a warning from the center of the square. "Don't listen to them! Come here!"

"What we have is much stronger than alcohol," the tallest said, maintaining her lock on two of the boys.

Gertie was impressed by the way the three were able to manipulate all six into following them around the corner and into an alleyway. Gertie followed, too, reminding the others telepathically that the humans must be willing.

Stay out of this, the tallest said to Gertie.

Under the spell of the vampires, the six college students lined up, side by side, with their backs against a building in the shadows where even the moonlight did not reach. The three vampires caressed their cheeks and smoothed their hair and told the students they were about to receive unimaginable power. They were also told that they should return here, night after night, if they wished to continue to receive this magnificent gift.

Then the vampires sank their teeth into the necks and wrists of their victims. Gertie licked her lips. The college students fell back against the wall and gazed into the night sky with the illusion of drinking a purple liquid from crystal goblets. The vampire virus first paralyzed them and then made them dizzy with pleasure. In a few moments, the three vampires abandoned their victims after having taken a pint, or more, from each of them. They said nothing to Gertie as they left.

After a few moments of disorientation, smiles unanimously spread across the faces of the students. They held hands and danced, sang some kind of European rap song, and then ran around the alley like children high on sugar. All six students believed they were hallucinating when one of them began to hover a few feet from the ground.

"What the?" her friend below squealed. "How are you doing that?"

"I dunno," the boy said. "I just felt like I was flying, from the elixir, you know. Then suddenly…." He dropped off and laughed as he wobbled in the air.

Feeling responsible for them, and curious, too, Gertie followed the students as they ran screaming with glee like trains through the streets. As soon as they realized they really could fly, they took to the sky, gliding just above the buildings. They laughed with hysteria when one of them had the idea of making loop-de-loops and they all followed suit. Their laughter was contagious. Soon Gertie was overcome with the giggles.

The laughter ended when one of them crashed into the side of a building and broke her neck. It was the same girl who had skinned her knees. She slid down the side of the building and landed on the street in traffic. The screech of brakes from a yellow cab screamed along with Gertie and the students as the cab drove over the girl.

"Oh my effing God!" one of the girls cried as they clumsily landed on the sidewalk near their friend. "Oh my effing God!"

"Alyssa!" One of the boys charged into the street and knelt beside the body, afraid to touch it.

Gertie moved nearer, wondering if she should do something. Should she try to get help? The girl was dying. Her blood had pooled onto the street.

Gertie hated herself for thinking of the blood as wasted food, but there it was.

"Alyssa?"

The girl didn't move.

The other two boys were each on a cell phone trying to get help. The two girls were crying. No other mortals dared leave the center of the square or the safety of the bars and cafes. They knew vampires were lurking.

And they were. Gertie sensed them moving in. They all wanted some of the luscious blood spilling from the girl's neck and skull.

Making herself invisible, Gertie stripped from her new clothes, swooped in, and took four full drags from the dying girl's neck before flying off in shame.

She was already dying, she told herself all the way back to the island through her tears of shame.

All the next day, Jeno held her in his arms while she cried for the girl who had died.

A week later, after she and Jeno had returned from Athens and while they were walking hand in hand along the coast of the island she had come to call Alexander (so as to master the hurtful memory and not allow it to master her), Jeno whisked her up in his arms without warning and lifted her up into the night sky.

She couldn't read his thoughts, which meant his mind was guarded, and yet he wore a smile on his face.

"I want to give you something," he said.

"What is it?" She couldn't imagine what he would have to give her. All of his possessions had been destroyed, except the very few they had salvaged.

He reached his hands behind his neck and removed his sister's locket. He had worn it since the day she had died. "I want you to have it."

"Jeno, I…"

He leaned over and put it on her. "I can appreciate it better by seeing it on you. Please wear it. For me."

She clasped the locket to her throat and nodded. "Of course."

"There's an inscription inside." He opened the locket and read, "*Happiness is a choice that requires effort.* Aeschylus said that."

"I like it. It's really deep."

"And true. Calandra tried to live by that idea. She worked hard at finding happiness."

"Thank you, Jeno. This is very sweet of you." She kissed him.

Two weeks after the attack on the acropolis, Jeno took Gertie to a supplier in the Angelis neighborhood, and she couldn't resist taking the opportunity to peek inside their living-room window. She was astonished by what she saw.

Mamá had strung popcorn into garland for their scraggily Christmas tree, and Klaus and Nikita were draping it over the branches while Phoebe added homemade ornaments. Babá topped the tree with a white, glittery star. As Gertie read their minds, she was overjoyed to learn that each of them was thinking of her and of how much they wished she was there with them. Nikita had even made her something and had wrapped it and put it under the tree. Tears blurred Gertie's vampire vision as she fought the urge to burst in and say, "Here I am!"

She didn't have to fight that urge long, because soon she heard a knock at their door and nearly fell out of the sky when the person who entered was her very own mother.

Sensing her shock and anxiety, Jeno put an arm around Gertie's waist. "It's going to be okay," he whispered.

Together, they watched the scene unfold.

"What did they say?" Mamá asked, rushing to Gertie's mother.

Gertie had forgotten how tall and curvy her mother was, and her hair, though dyed to cover the gray, was the same color blonde as Gertie's. Her mother's stylish cut, fashionable clothes, and stiletto heels made her look out of place in the tiny apartment.

"They promised to do what they can," Gertie's mother replied.

Gertie read their minds to learn that her mother had just returned from Hector's house, where she had met with Hector, his mother, and a group of other demigods.

"Oh, Diane, please, sit down with me here on the sofa and tell me all about it," Mamá said, putting an arm around her friend and sitting close beside her.

Gertie was astounded by the thoughts running through each woman's mind. Mamá was beyond worried, in a near state of panic, and on the verge of leading an army to destroy every vampire in sight in order to save Gertie and bring her home.

Gertie's mother's thoughts were mixed and more complicated. She was frightened but resigned. She'd never really allowed herself to consider Gertie hers.

What? Gertie tried to dig further into her mother's thoughts. Without eye contact, it was difficult to get past all the swirling ideas—everything from *this room is so small and this couch is so uncomfortable* to *is that a roach on the ceiling?*

"Why would my mother never allow herself to think of me as her daughter?" Gertie muttered. "That makes no sense."

"I thought he would claim her by now," Gertie's mother said. "Why hasn't he come forward? Has he forgotten, do you think?"

"Who can tell the intentions of the gods?" Mamá said.

Klaus and Nikita exchanged looks of surprise, but both refrained from asking the question that had popped into each of their minds: *Gertie is the daughter of a god?*

Gertie's own mind was spinning now. "I think I'm going to be sick. Do vampires vomit?"

"Not usually, I don't think." Jeno tightened his hold on her.

"Why would he command me to return her before her eighteenth birthday only to allow her to become a vampire?" her mother asked.

Her mother knew she was a vampire?

"What have I done, Marta?" Gertie's mother sank into the sofa and covered her face.

"This isn't your fault," Mamá said. "You did what you thought was best. He told you to send her here, no?"

"That's what he said." Gertie's mother broke into tears. "That was seventeen years ago. Maybe he's forgotten. Maybe I was a fool to believe his threats."

Babá cleared his throat. "I'm going to take the kids around the corner for some yogurt."

"It's too dangerous at this time of night," Mamá objected.

"I'll be careful. Children, get your coats."

"No, I'm the one who should leave," Gertie's mother said. "I'll go back to my hotel."

"I wish you would stay here with us," Mamá said.

Gertie's mother stood up and went to the door. "Nonsense. I don't want to impose."

Her mother's real reason for not wanting to stay was that she was too repulsed to sleep in the tiny, roach-infested apartment.

"No need to go so soon, Diane," Babá insisted. "The children and I will be fine just around the corner. It's dark but early yet."

Diane moved away from the door as Babá led all three kids from the apartment. Gertie held her breath and watched the steps in front of their apartment building. Unable to resist, she flew down to the street and waited.

"Are you sure this is a good idea?" Jeno came up behind her.

"No. But I want to say hello."

Nikita was the first to notice her as they descended the steps toward the sidewalk. "Gertie?" She ran down the remaining steps and practically knocked Gertie over, the same way she had done in the station the evening they had first met.

Gertie was filled with joy, and she hugged Nikita close to her and kissed the side of her cheek. The aroma of her blood filled Gertie's nostrils, but she ignored it to relish in the delight of being with her best friend—her sister.

"Nikita, no!" Babá cried. In a few moments he was at her side, pulling her away from Gertie. "She's changed. We can no longer trust her."

"That's not true." Gertie clung to Nikita's hands. "I haven't changed, really. I'm the same person on the inside." She pulled Nikita close to her again. "I miss you. All of you." Tears welled in her eyes. She could see them in Nikita's too.

Babá grabbed Nikita's arm and pulled her away. Gertie was tempted to use mind control to keep them there with her, but she was afraid it would backfire as it had the last time she had tried it on them. Babá's mind was full of fear. He was terrified for his family and terrified of her and Jeno, and she didn't want to add to those fears.

"I'm sorry," Gertie said to him. "I didn't mean to frighten you, Babá."

He averted his eyes. "Don't call me that."

Gertie blanched. Mortified that the man she thought of as a father could be so harsh, she took a step back and glanced up at Klaus, who stood beside Phoebe on the front steps. Klaus's mind was also full of fear—and also of a deep hatred directed at Jeno.

"I miss you, too," Nikita said through her tears as Babá dragged her away. "And don't worry," she called out. "Hector will help you. Your mother is here, and she's…"

"Enough, Nikita!" Babá demanded as they turned the corner and disappeared from sight.

But Gertie could still hear their thoughts, and Nikita's were hopeful. She had faith that Hector and the other demigods would save her.

Gertie felt the blood from her recent feeding rush to her cheeks as she turned to Jeno. "I don't want to be saved," she reminded him.

"That won't stop them from trying."

She read his thoughts of betrayal by a family he had once risked his life to help. At Marta's pleading, Jeno had changed her dying two-year old, Damien, into a vampire, even though Jeno had tried to talk her out of it. Not only had they felt no gratitude for Jeno, but now they wanted his father dead.

Gertie tried to think of something comforting to say.

"Don't even try. Let's go."

Gertie flew up to the window once more to look in at Mamá and her mother. She had once believed that seeing her mother might make her feel differently about wanting to live with the Angelis family, but it didn't—though reading her mother's mind took the edge off of Gertie's feelings of abandonment. Her mother had never allowed herself to think of Gertie as her own. The man Gertie had believed was her father wasn't. That explained so much—their self-absorbed lives hadn't been a consequence of Gertie's un-lovability or of her parents' disappointment in her. It had more to do with their own perception of themselves as temporary caretakers. But it also created new questions, and Diane's complicated and confused mind answered none of them.

Gertie left the window feeling even worse than she had felt when she had first looked in.

No, that wasn't exactly true. The hug from Nikita had filled Gertie with enough joy to make the whole horrible night worth it.

Plus, she had learned something important about herself.

She was the daughter of a god. That was so hard to comprehend. Nikita had once said that most humans were descendants of gods, so it was just a matter of the degree of separation. From what Gertie had read, Prometheus, one of the Titans had made humankind out of clay. Nikita had said that, while that was true, the gods didn't seem able to resist mating with mortals, so most people had a bit of the divine running through them. What made a human a demigod was having a *parent* who was a god. Those with a divine grandparent may have some special talents, but they weren't considered demigods and didn't serve with Hector and the others as warriors for the Olympians.

Gertie struggled with the news that she was a demigod, that her actual father was an actual god. Which one? Her mother didn't seem to know.

As she and Jeno flew across the sea toward Alexander, she tried to think of any characteristics she possessed that might hint at the identity of her father, but she could think of none. She loved to read, loved to learn about mythology and lore, kept to herself, was not quick to make friends, and was pretty much a loner and an outsider. She had no special talents. She wasn't artistic, couldn't sing, couldn't heal (like Hector), wasn't particularly strong or fast or athletic (before becoming a vampire), and had no affinity for the water (like Percy Jackson). Gertie didn't possess a single special quality.

That's not true. Jeno said in her mind. *Your love and compassion set you apart.*

"Thank you, Jeno." She kissed his cheek. "But that doesn't help, unless Aphrodite is my father."

Jeno chuckled and squeezed her hand.

Maybe Gertie's father was just some jerk who had tricked her mother into believing he was a god. But then why would he tell her she'd have to return Gertie to Greece before her eighteenth birthday?

When they arrived at the island south of Athens, they found an amazing sight. In the middle of a circle of at least two hundred vampires, a golden ram stood with a troupe of women and satyrs. The vampires' prayers had been answered: their lord had come.

<u>CHAPTER SEVEN</u>

The Dance

Gertie followed Jeno to his father's side within the circle of vampires gathered around their lord, Dionysus. The Maenads and satyrs were quiet and still as they listened to the booming voice emanating from the golden ram.

"I hear the cries of the disenfranchised," the god said. "I am nothing if not the god of the exiled. It has been my great hope to one day usher the children of the night into liberty. We will begin tonight."

The crowd roared with excitement but quieted down again when the Maenads lifted their pine-cone-tipped torches. Gertie recognized Jeno's mother among the leather-clad Maenads. Her dark hair was thick and fluffy, like Jeno's, but even longer and wilder, like a shaggy black carpet draped over her head and down her back. Her dark eyes were fierce and without emotion or recognition. Gertie squeezed Jeno's hands as she read the flood of memories his mother's presence brought to him.

"We will invade Athens tonight," the god continued. "Let it be understood that we must start by increasing our army. You, my children of the night, must make more vampires."

Gertie whispered, "That won't solve anything. It will only get us all killed."

The golden ram turned in her direction, as though he had heard her. Gertie held her breath.

"Do I sense a dissenter among you?" Dionysus demanded.

He *had* heard her. She wished she could disappear.

"Come forward, then, and state your objection so that *all* can hear."

Gertie clung to Jeno. "I don't want to. Help me. Say something."

Jeno moved forward in her place to face the golden ram in the center of the circle. "I meant no disrespect, my lord."

"You are not the one whose voice I heard. Bring the girl to me."

Gertie wanted to run when Jeno turned to her with frightened eyes, but she moved to the center of the crowd to stand beside Jeno before the enormous golden ram.

"What's your name?" the god asked.

"Gertrude Morgan."

"And what is your objection?"

She shifted her weight nervously from one foot to the other. "I don't believe the other gods will respond the way you think they will to an increased number of vampires."

"No? And your belief is based on what? You have a relationship with the gods? Or you can read their minds, little vampire?"

Snickering burst out among the crowd.

"No. Nothing like that."

Say "my lord" when you speak to him, Jeno advised.

I can't. It doesn't feel right.

"Then what?" Dionysus asked.

"Well, I've read lots of stories about them."

"Stories?" the ram laughed. "She's read stories."

More laughter rang out.

"Written by Homer and Euripides," she added quickly, trying to defend herself. She hated being laughed at. "Stories about great gods and great heroes, including stories about you. And I'm telling you I may be just a *little vampire*, but even I can see that your plan is wrong. The gods will feel justified in destroying us if we go against their laws and increase our number. They already hate us and are looking for a reason to exterminate us from the earth. Just look at what Athena did at the acropolis."

An explosion of murmurs shot from the crowd until the Maenads lifted their pine-cone-tipped torches. The other vampires hadn't heard that Athena had been behind the destruction of their homes.

"If we want change, we need leverage," Gertie said.

The golden ram took several heavy steps in the sand toward her, so that she stood directly beneath him. He sniffed her and said, "And how do you suppose we gain leverage?"

"We take something important from them as a bargaining tool—at least, that's how it's done in the stories."

Gertie had been so nervous that she'd been unable to read any of the thoughts of those around her, including Jeno's. She took in a deep breath and tried to control her shaky hands and limbs. Despite her anxiety, she had no regrets. It felt good to stand up and speak her mind. She knew she was right. She only hoped she could be taken seriously enough to convince the others.

"Who is your father?" Dionysus asked.

Gertie hung her head, her feelings of confidence diminishing. "I don't know."

After a few moments of painful silence, the golden ram said, "Yes. The little vampire is right."

Gertie turned to Jeno, who smiled back at her. She could now read his thoughts of relief as he threw his arms around her and kissed the side of her face. He had been worried that Gertie would be ripped apart by the Maenads as punishment for contradicting the god. He took her hand and kissed it.

"We need leverage," Dionysus said. "As I consider what that will be, let's celebrate the beginning of our uprising with a dance. Drink my wine, children of the night! For, though it will not quench your thirst and give you sustenance like blood, it will liberate you from your current anxiety and purge you of grief. Satyrs! Play upon your pipes! Maenads! Pass around the golden cups!"

Within seconds, the beach thundered with the vigorous music of the satyrs, who hopped from hoof to hoof as they played, turning in circles and engaging the vampires in their dance. Jeno pulled Gertie away from the center of the circle, but Gertie resisted.

"Let's have fun," she said. "I want to dance in the crowd for a change."

"You don't dance, remember?" he said, his memories of the fall dance washing over her.

"You're a good enough dancer for both of us, *remember*?"

Jeno smiled. "As you wish, but don't drink the wine, okay?"

"Why not? It won't turn me into a…"

"Vampires aren't affected that way."

"Then what's the harm in one sip?"

He raked his hand through his thick hair—a gesture she'd seen his father do. "Nothing, as long as one sip doesn't become several cups."

Gertie laughed and shook her head. "Another lecture about being a responsible vampire. What are you? My father?"

"No. But I might just have to spank you." He gave her a wicked smile that filled her with happiness.

Before she could think of a reply, a satyr handed her a goblet. She took a sip and passed it to Jeno, who did the same. One sip was all it took to make her head spin. Suddenly, she was a little girl, alone in her backyard behind her parents' giant mansion, spinning round and round, arms out, like the propellers of a helicopter.

When books hadn't been enough to exorcise her demons, she'd spin and spin until she fell down in the grass and watched the world revolving around her.

She fell on the sand and gazed at the stars, spinning above her in the sky. They moved so fast they resembled comets. Her mother used to say the world didn't revolve around Gertie. What a mean thing to say to a child she rarely spent time with. But Gertie would run out to the backyard and spin and spin and then laugh at the proof in the sky: the world *did* revolve around Gertie. And it revolved around her now.

She was overcome with laughter, from deep behind her diaphragm. It shook her like a carnival ride. Life could be so ridiculous. The world was so ridiculous. Everyone was mad and everything was nonsensical. Who cared about this world? She didn't. Let her get lost in a glass of wine!

No! She meant *book*. She laughed at herself. Not a glass of wine, a book! Let her get lost in a book. Isn't that what she did? Isn't that how she coped with being unloved by her parents? Isn't that how she dealt with feeling like an outsider in her own school? Books had become her liberation, her ecstasy, her wine!

She sat up, suddenly sobered, and scanned the beach for Jeno. He was dancing with his mother and father! His mother was still clearly unaware of their relationship to her, but the father and son seemed not to care. They wore smiles of glee, and in their drunken stupor, were, at least temporarily, happy.

Gertie resisted the urge to run to them and break them from their reverie with the news of her revelation. She knew who her father was— at least she had a very strong suspicion. In fact, as the music resounded and the world continued to spin, she had a strange vision of him protecting her with his thick golden vines. But now that she knew, did she want anyone else to know?

CHAPTER EIGHT

Warnings and Betrayal

Gertie tried to sleep most of the next day curled in a corner of the cave in Jeno's arms, but strange dreams kept waking her.

She dreamt she was in a dark forest and her parents, along with Jeno's mother and father and the college student who had died, were ripping her limbs from her body and laughing at her. Dionysus stood as a golden ram looking down at them and was laughing the loudest.

Over and over, the same dream haunted her, until at last the setting changed from forest to sea.

Then Hector appeared before her and everyone else fell away. Her limbs were intact, and she was treading water in the sea beneath a full moon. Hector took her in his arms and kissed her, like that night she had thought she'd been hallucinating. Her hands ran over his muscular body and tugged at his wet hair. She wrapped her legs around his waist. His lips moved to her throat. Tears of joy streamed down her cheeks as she whispered his name.

She awoke with Hector's name on her lips. Had she said it out loud? She immediately shielded her mind to protect Jeno's feelings, but he was awake and smiling at her like someone who has found peace with bad news.

"Are you okay, koureetsi mou?"

She nodded and rubbed her eyes. "You?"

"Last night was a big night for you. First learning about your father, and then being singled out by Dionysus in front of everyone." He stroked her hair. "Are you sure you're okay? What are you guarding from me?"

"I think I know who my father is," she blurted out, in an effort to distract him from the truth.

"Oh?"

"But I'm not ready to tell anyone, in case I'm wrong. Can you understand that?"

"Of course." He kissed the tip of her nose. "Take your time. We have all the time in the world."

Sometime later, Vladimir came and sat with them. He told Jeno what he remembered of Calandra, when they were children, before the Maenads. He also shared what he had been able to sense about their lives from his tomb.

"I could sometimes hear her singing," Vladimir said. "I had to concentrate very hard, but when she was in the caves beneath the acropolis, I could sometimes hear her."

"She had a beautiful voice," Jeno said.

Gertie remained quiet and wished she could disappear to give the men their privacy.

"I'm thankful you have joined us," Vladimir said to Gertie, shocking her. "I've lost a beloved daughter, but it comforts me to know I have gained another one in you."

"Thank you," she said, trying very hard to block her mind, which had wandered off to Babá and the Angelis family.

That night, after feeding in Athens, she and Jeno returned to the beach of Alexander just as the other vampires were gathering for another meeting. Although the golden ram and his entourage of Maenads and satyrs were not present, Vladimir was addressing the crowd—which had grown in number to at least three hundred.

Jeno and Gertie picked their way through the crowd toward the center of the ring where Vladimir stood, with Homer and Euripides on either side of him, insisting that their lord, Dionysus, had appeared to him in a dream.

"I do not want to be overheard," Vladimir said. "So I invite each and every one of you into my mind."

Gertie focused in on Vladimir's thoughts. After navigating through some strange images of Dionysus in human form and half naked, she found the vein of Vladimir's thought pattern: To gain leverage against the gods of Mount Olympus, the vampires must go after their warriors on earth.

"Their warriors on earth?" she whispered to Jeno, but before he replied, she'd figured it out on her own: the demigods.

Hector.

Gertie gasped. Was this *her* doing? She was the one who had told Dionysus they needed to gain leverage, but she was thinking about Zeus's lightning bolt or Hades's helm of invisibility, like in *Percy Jackson*, or Poseidon's trident, like in *The Gatekeeper's Saga*. She hadn't meant *people*! Oh, why couldn't she have just kept her mouth shut? She had to warn Hector. But if she took off now across the night sky, the others would notice.

She closed her eyes and prayed to the god she believed was her father. *Please don't do this. I am your daughter, I think, and I beg of you to gain your leverage in some other way. Let me steal the helm from Hades or the trident from Poseidon.*

If Dionysus heard her, he gave no sign.

Vladimir telepathically shared with them his plan for locating the demigods. The vampires would have to cull them out by destroying human life, out in the open. Then, when the demigods responded to the blatant breach of law, they would be ambushed.

Gertie was horrified. They weren't just going to *capture* people; they were going to *kill* people, too.

She tried once more to pray to Dionysus, but, once again, she had no sense of her words being heard.

"We can't let them do this," she whispered to Jeno.

"Keep your thoughts to yourself, and keep your mind heavily guarded," he warned, as he tenderly kissed the top of her head.

"Promise me you'll help me steer everyone clear of the Angelis family," she whispered.

"I promise," Jeno replied.

Over the next few hours, Vladimir divided the army into squadrons based on their existing clans and assigned them the major cities of Greece. With roughly thirty members to a clan, they formed eleven squadrons and were assigned cities as north as Thessaloniki, as east as Rhodes, as south as Heraklion, and as west as Corfu. Vladimir encouraged everyone to familiarize themselves with their territory tonight and be prepared to strike tomorrow night. The demigods were to be taken—alive—to the Minotaur's labyrinth, where Dionysus would be waiting.

"I wonder why Dionysus wouldn't first have us recruit more vampires," Gertie whispered. "Most of us are from Athens. There are bound to be others."

"Less than a hundred of us are from Athens."

"Even so."

"Maybe he wants to protect the element of surprise by attacking quickly."

"Hmm." That didn't help her, though. The longer she could put off the attack, the more time she'd have to warn Hector.

Gertie and Jeno belonged to Vladimir's squadron, and to Gertie's profound relief, their assigned city was Athens. Maybe she could protect her family after all. Because it was their hometown, Vladimir did not take his squadron into the city to scout that night. Instead, they remained on the beach to pray and to further strategize.

Carefully guarding her mind, Gertie told Jeno she needed to feed again. It wasn't unusual for her to make a second trip back to Athens before dawn for more blood, but she couldn't avoid raising his suspicions.

"I'll go with you, koureetsi mou," he offered.

"That's okay. You stay and help your father. I won't be gone long."

He wrapped his arms around her waist and gazed deeply into her eyes. "I know you are conflicted. I don't blame you."

Her heart raced in her chest. She couldn't *fool* Jeno. Why was she trying? "I want to protect my family."

"*We* are your family now, no? You are a vampire, and unless you're willing to kill my father, you will remain a vampire. The sooner you accept this fact, the better for all of us."

"You promised you would help me protect them."

"I will, when the time comes. But there's no need to warn them."

She closed her eyes, keeping her mind blocked. His was blocked as well.

"Sometimes it takes painful sacrifices to create change," he said. "I don't like the idea of killing humans any more than you do. We can minimize the death toll if we all work together. It will all be over soon."

"And what if it isn't?"

Jeno pointed a finger at her. "I know my father. He doesn't kill with pleasure."

"We need to stand up to him and to Dionysus. We need to tell him this is wrong."

"Is it wrong?"

"Killing people for any reason is wrong."

"History disagrees with you."

"I need to feed." She pulled away from him and turned toward the sea.

"I know why you want to go to Athens."

The little bit of blood pumping through her veins rushed to her cheeks as she turned to him and said, "He's my friend."

"And my enemy." His face also turned red. "Not by *my* choice. *He* is the one who threatened my family. I did nothing but protect his."

"Until you changed me."

He blanched. "That was an accident."

"But you weren't thinking of me." Tears welled in her eyes.

"Must I always think of you?"

She spoke through gritted teeth. "You put me in harm's way without hesitation."

"You wouldn't have been in harm's way had you not begged me to drink from you so often, had you not lusted for my power." He struggled to maintain his composure. "I lost track of how much of your blood I'd consumed. I never wanted it."

"Yes, you did."

"You are as much to blame as I."

She wanted to scream. "I didn't know I would be used to awaken your father, to instigate all of this…"

"Watch what you say out loud."

"Please don't follow me." She lifted off the ground.

He snapped his hand around her wrist. "Gertie, wait. Please. I love you."

"I love you, too." She jerked her hand free and took off across the sea, streaming tears.

When she reached Hector's house, she was surprised to find his upstairs window open, even though it was winter. Across the room beyond his bed, Hector sat at his desk with a charcoal pencil. His thoughts revealed that he was drawing her again. She cringed when she saw the image through his eyes. He had portrayed her as a vampire with sharp fangs dripping with blood. Her arms were raised in a threatening gesture.

So that was what she was to him now: a monster.

As tears fell down her cheeks, he sensed her and met her eyes with shock.

"Gertie?" He jumped from his chair and was at the window in less than a second. "I'm so glad to see you. Come in."

"I can't stay. I've come to warn you."

"Come in, please."

She flew inside and looked up at him, resisting the urge to wrap her arms around his neck. He was shirtless, in nothing but a pair of blue pajama pants. He looked beautiful and had the sweetest smile on his face. Unable to resist reading his thoughts, she learned how badly he wished to kiss her.

"Hector, I…"

He took her in his arms and held her close, his cheek pressed against the top of her head. "I've been worried sick about you."

She inhaled his scent and sighed. How she wished she could stay there, enfolded in his arms, her face nestled against his chest. She glanced at the window, on the lookout for Jeno and the others. They could be coming at any moment.

Hector cupped her face and pressed his lips to her cheek, and she felt like melting candle wax.

Oh my gods, his mind said to hers, echoing her sentiments exactly.

"I'm so sorry, Hector. I never meant for this to happen. I was trying to help."

"I know. Tell me how you've been. Are you doing okay? I've been mad with worry."

"I've been okay. I miss everyone." She hadn't meant to cry again, but the tears came uncontrollably. "I miss Mamá and Babá and Nikita and everyone."

Have you missed me?

"Of course, I've missed you, too."

He kissed her other cheek, and she thought she would melt away. Being in his arms made her feel dizzy with pleasure and made her want to forget about everything else.

But she couldn't allow herself to forget. Lives were at stake. "Hector, I…"

Hector closed the window. "It's friggin' cold out there tonight."

She read his mind again and learned he had only kept the window open with the hope of her return. Now that she was here, he could close it.

But she knew closing it would not protect them from the vampires if Jeno had decided to follow, either alone or with others from their squadron.

"Listen to me, Hector," she said, trying to focus on her reason for coming. "The vampires are planning to capture demigods from all the major cities of Greece tomorrow night."

"What?"

"Their plan is to kill innocent people out in the open to cull the demigods out. Then the vampires will ambush the demigods and take them to the Minotaur's labyrinth."

"But why?"

"To use you as leverage. They want the gods' cooperation." Her stomach felt sick at the thought that she was responsible for planting the idea of leverage in Dionysus's mind. Her stomach also hurt because she was hungry. She needed blood.

"For what? What do they hope to gain from all this?"

"Freedom."

Hector's brows furled. "Freedom? They aren't prisoners. I don't understand."

"It's the way they're treated, how they're looked down upon, even by the gods. They want respect and economic freedom."

"*Economic* freedom? What's stopping them from that?"

"They can't get jobs because people look down on them. They want to be able to own their own homes instead of having to hide out in caves." She thought of the women who slummed in the city. "Many of them really do have pathetic lives."

"But they're a danger to society, Gertie. We can't have them living among us."

"Only because they're desperate. And many of them already live among humans. If we organized some kind of blood bank for them, if we made it easier for them to survive…"

"Are you serious?"

She gawked at him. "You do realize I'm one of them now."

"Not for long."

"But…." The idea of becoming human again filled her with hope. As much as she loved Jeno and sympathized with the other vampires, she missed her humanity. But did she miss it enough to destroy Vladimir?

"I've got to warn the others," Hector said.

"How?"

He grabbed his cell phone from his desk. "I'll text every demigod I know. We can meet tomorrow at our council hall to discuss what to do."

Gertie hoped she'd done the right thing. The vampires wouldn't stand a chance if the demigods and gods united forces.

Of course, she'd done the right thing. How could she question it? The vampires planned to destroy human lives. She just felt so sorry for Jeno and for all he had lost. And she really did understand why the vampires wanted change.

When he finished his text, Hector's phone rang. It was his mother. Gertie could hear through the phone. His mother said she was at the hospital and couldn't talk but she would be at the meeting. She also wanted to know if he'd seen Gertie.

"She's with me now."

"Don't let her leave. The tramps will want to destroy her once they learn what she's done."

"Got it."

Gertie was overcome with fear. She hadn't given any thought about what would happen to her by coming here; she'd known only that she had to come.

Hector returned the phone to his desk and took Gertie in his arms. "Don't worry. I'll protect you with my life."

"That's what worries me. I came to warn you, but I've just put you in even greater danger, if what your mother says is true."

"She's only speculating."

"I should go."

"That's crazy. I don't want you to ever leave my side again."

"I know you want to protect me, but…"

"This is about more than that. You know how I feel. Please don't leave and break my heart again."

"I promise to come back," Gertie said. "I'll be right back."

Hector squeezed her shoulders. "Are you kidding? I'm afraid to let you out of my sight. Let me go with you."

"But I need to…." She didn't want to say it, especially after the picture he'd been drawing of her.

"You need blood?"

Hesitantly, she nodded.

"Drink from *me*." He leaned in, as though he would kiss her. "Take *my* blood."

"Hector, I…"

"Please."

He pressed his lips to hers, and every cell in her body rejoiced. Then he bit his tongue and slipped it between her lips.

She wasn't sure if it was because he was a demigod or because she was falling in love with him, but the taste of his blood was rich and delicious—more so than that of any other she had tasted. She gently sucked on his tongue, but it only made her thirstier.

As if he had read her mind, he lifted his chin to expose his neck. She kissed the soft skin where it pulsed. She licked and kissed along his throat, going crazy with the thoughts coming from his mind. He knew it wasn't the right time, but he was fighting the desire to feel every part of her body with his hands, to touch her skin with every part of his.

She gasped with the conflicting desires coursing through her body. She wanted to drink, but she also wanted to crash her body against his to never be separated again.

Quenching one desire over another, she moved her hands along his back, around his waist, and up his chest to his shoulders and biceps, thoroughly enjoying the sensation of his growing desire for her.

He pressed his lips hard against hers. She twisted her fingers through his hair, unable to stop the moan from escaping her throat. His hands cupped her bottom and lifted her off the floor. She wrapped her legs around his waist, like she had in the dream.

"Oh, Hector," she whispered in between kisses.

"I love you, Gertie," he said against her mouth. "I love you so much."

Dare she admit it? She'd known for a long time. "I love you, too."

Her mouth stretched open as her fangs extended of their own accord. She opened her eyes and flinched at the sight of Jeno watching through Hector's window. He'd made himself invisible, but she, of course, could see him perfectly. His mind was unguarded. He wanted her to read his hurt and misery and feelings of betrayal as she closed her eyes and sank her fangs into Hector's throat.

Jeno spoke telepathically to her as she drank Hector's sweet blood. *If you want to come back with me, I won't tell the others what you've done.*

I'm sorry, Jeno. I can't. She kept her eyes closed, fighting to hold back tears as she drew the warm, rich sustenance from Hector.

That hurts so much more than I imagined it would.

I tried my best to love you, but it wasn't enough. Her throat tightened at that thought, but the blood found its way down.

I will protect you from the others as best as I can.

He was too good to her. He didn't deserve her betrayal. *I don't expect you to help me after what I've done.*

I can't betray my father. I will defend and support him.

Oh, Jeno. I understand. My sweet, Jeno. I'm so sorry.

I will always love you, koureetsi mou. And if you ever change your mind…Just remember, immortality is a long time. Maybe someday, things will be different, and you and I will have a chance.

Not wanting to weaken Hector, Gertie drank no more than one pint. She licked her lips and looked once more at Jeno before he sadly turned and flew away.

Gertie pressed her face into Hector's chest and wept.

CHAPTER NINE

Taken by Surprise

The hot water of the shower comforted Gertie and mingled with her tears. She would never forget the look on Jeno's face at Hector's window. It had made her feel like someone had driven a stake through her heart.

As she rinsed the shampoo from her hair, she thought again of how Babá had glared at her with fear and disgust and had told her not to call him Babá anymore.

The man she had once believed was her father—James Morgan—was nothing to her and had never loved her.

The god she now believed was her father seemed not to care for her either.

And the man who had offered to be like a father to her—Vladimir—would have to be destroyed if she were to ever be human again.

Life was so unfair.

Gertie wished she could get lost in a book.

Hector had given Gertie back her things, which she had left behind at his house. It felt good to wear her old pajamas and to brush her teeth and comb her hair. In the side pocket of her bag was her e-reader. Yes, she would get lost in a book.

When she left the guest bathroom, she searched for Hector's thoughts, but couldn't find him. She went down the hall, looking for him in his bedroom, though she had hoped he would stay the night with her because she was scared and didn't want to be alone. When she didn't find him, she became alarmed.

She searched the entire house—upstairs, downstairs, and even the basement. He was nowhere to be found. As she was about to go into full panic mode, she sensed his presence just before he walked through the front door.

"Where were you?" she asked.

"I'm sorry. I really thought I'd be back before you finished showering."

"Where did you go?"

"To my father's temple. I flew, since…you know."

She blushed. "You could have been captured."

"It was worth the risk. He came."

"Hephaestus?"

Hector nodded, smiling. "He promised to talk to Zeus and Athena and the other gods of Olympus. He won't let us fight this battle alone."

"Did you tell him what the vampires want? Did you ask him to help liberate them?"

"What?" Hector frowned. "No."

"Why not?"

"I guess I was more concerned with protecting human life."

Gertie narrowed her eyes. "See, that's the problem. Humans and gods don't value the lives of vampires. Until they do, things will never change. I can't believe I came here. I can't believe I abandoned them."

She flew back up the stairs to the guest room, with Hector on her heels saying, "Wait, Gertie…"

She slammed the door in his face.

I need to be alone, she told him telepathically.

Please, Gertie. You just got here. I'm so sorry. I should have thought of that. I'm so stupid.

She blocked her mind and went for her salvation—her e-reader. It wasn't charged, so she plugged it in near the bed and climbed beneath the covers. Not in the mood to read the next book in *The Vampire Chronicles*, she searched for something else. She needed a fairy tale with a happy ending.

Gertie must have fallen asleep at some point while she'd been reading, for the scorching light of dawn bearing in on her through the window awakened her. She moaned and rolled off the bed into its shadow. She caught her breath and listened for Hector's thoughts. She couldn't sense him or his mother. Maybe they were at the council meeting.

She felt along the top of the mattress for her e-reader, tolerating the pain of the sun on her hand. Finding the device, she brought it into the shadows with her and searched for the place where she had left off in her book. It felt good to get lost in a story and forget all that was going on. She read all morning, until the shadow of the bed became too narrow, and then she rolled beneath the bed and kept reading.

Sometime later, she heard the front door and sensed Hector's mother running up the stairs.

"Gertie?" She opened the guest room door. "Are you here?"

"Under the bed." Gertie held her e-reader out in the light.

Hector's mother knelt down and pressed her cheek to the floor. "Hi, I'm Dori, Hector's mother," she said without smiling. "Hector's missing. Do you know where he is?"

"Missing?" Gertie bumped her head on the bottom of the bed. "He wasn't at the council meeting?"

"No. And he hasn't answered my text or calls."

"I haven't seen him since last night," Gertie said. "He'd gone to his father's temple."

"You haven't seen him since?"

"Yes. He came back. But…"

"But what?"

"I got upset with him. Oh, God. This is my fault."

"Where do you think he went?"

"Maybe he went back to his father's temple."

"Okay. I'll search there. Thanks." Dori climbed to her feet. "Would you mind telling me why you were upset with him?"

Gertie sighed. "He'd gone to ask his father for help in battle, but I thought he should have asked him to help liberate the vampires."

"I see."

"If the gods would only help them, maybe we could avoid a war."

"Thank you for telling me. I'll be back as soon as I can."

Dori hastened from the room. Gertie couldn't resist reading the woman's thoughts. If Dori couldn't find Hector at the acropolis, she was going to go consult her father's oracle at Mount Parnassus.

Gertie balled her fists. Everything was falling down around her, and all she could do was lie there in the dark. Never had she felt so helpless.

When dusk finally fell, Gertie climbed from beneath the bed and changed into fresh jeans and a knit top, wondering the whole time why neither Hector nor his mother had returned. The vampires would be attacking the cities soon, and, with or without Hector, Gertie planned to station herself near the Angelis apartment building. She was only one person, but she had to try her best to protect the people she loved.

Alone and frightened, she climbed from Hector's window, reaching out with her senses as far as she could stretch. She wished she had some clue as to where the vampires would strike. If the other demigods lived like Hector, then it was likely the vampires would strike in the suburbs. But an ambush might be easier in the city, where there were more places to hide.

Not wanting to draw attention to herself from other vampires, she took to the streets and ran, rather than flew, toward the inner city. By the time she reached the Angelis's apartment building, night had fallen, and so had a thick fog. Gertie flew up to the roof of the building, and, like a sentinel, prepared to wait.

As she looked in all directions for signs of the vampires, she sought Nikita's mind. Gertie was shocked to learn that Phoebe was missing. Gertie went from mind to mind. Phoebe had been taken from the building in the middle of the night. No one knew where she was.

Gertie paced on the rooftop, trying to think of what to do and wondering if Hector's disappearance had had anything to do with Phoebe's. No one in Nikita's family seemed to have any answers. Mamá hadn't stopped crying. Babá spoke on the phone with a local police officer. Gertie soon realized the officer was sitting in his patrol car across the street. She hoped he was a demigod, in case the vampires showed up.

When she could think of nothing else to do, Gertie prayed to the gods. "Please guide me. Show me what to do."

Suddenly it occurred to her that she could read Damien's mind. Since he had a psychic connection with Phoebe, maybe he could reveal what had happened to her. Gertie imagined the two-year-old vampire in his coffin in the basement, but when she reached out, she couldn't find him. She used her x-ray vision to look through the roof and through the three stories to the basement level. She scanned the basement for the tomb. When she found it, she gasped.

The lid was open, and the tomb was empty.

CHAPTER TEN

Damien and Phoebe

Gertie scrambled from the rooftop of the Angelis apartment building, flew into the first unlocked window she found, and rushed to the basement to see, firsthand, the open, empty tomb that belonged to Damien.

Mamá and Babá seemed unaware that Damien was missing, too. Hadn't anyone come looking here for Phoebe? If the police had searched for her here, the empty tomb would mean nothing to him. But wouldn't her parents have also searched in case Phoebe had come down to hide? No, of course not. Phoebe never went to the basement. Ever.

Gertie should tell them, shouldn't she? Wasn't it better for them to know, even if it would rip them apart with worry? If only she had a crystal ball to tell her what to do, or an oracle of Apollo, or anything.

They would blame Gertie for this and hate her even more than they already did. Tears streamed from her eyes as she imagined what they would say. But she had to tell them, anyway. It was the right thing to do.

She locked onto Mamá's mind: *Mamá, it's Gertie. Please don't be afraid. I have some bad news. Can you come to the basement?*

Gertie? Is this about Phoebe?

I think so. It seemed unlikely that Damien's disappearance was unrelated to Phoebe's.

Are you alone? Or are there others with you? Jeno?

I'm alone. I promise it's safe. I won't hurt you, Mamá. Please don't be frightened.

Gertie could sense how terrified Mamá was to go to the basement. She was scared of a trap. She was worried that Gertie was being used as bait to lure her into a nest of vampires. But her need to find her daughter propelled her down the stairs.

Mamá pulled the string over the basement steps, illuminating the otherwise dark room. Her trembling was painful for Gertie to watch.

"Mamá, it's okay," Gertie said. "It's just me. I won't hurt you. Please don't be afraid."

"Gertie?" Mamá's teeth were chattering with fear.

"I wanted you to see for yourself." Gertie pointed to Damien's open tomb. "Damien is gone. Whoever took him must have taken Phoebe, too."

Mamá covered her mouth with shaking hands. "Oh my heavens. Oh my heavens. My poor babies. You don't know where they are?"

Gertie shook her head. "I'm sorry."

"Oh my God. Please help me!" Mamá slumped onto the bottom step and covered her face.

Gertie dared to move closer to her. "I will do everything I can to bring them back to you. I promise." Tears streamed down her cheeks, and she, too, was trembling. "If I have to die to make it happen, I will. Please believe me."

Mamá looked up at her and then reached out her hands. "Come here, Gertoula."

Sobs literally shook Gertie's entire body as she fell into Mamá's embrace.

"Oh, my sweet Gertoula," Mamá said.

Gertie held on for dear life. "I'm so sorry, Mamá . I love you so much."

"And I love you, koureetsi mou. I've just been so frightened."

"I know. I promise to protect you and your family as best as I can."

Mamá stroked Gertie's hair. "I believe you. And thank you. You are my only hope of ever seeing my babies again."

As much as Gertie wished she could stay longer in Mamá's loving arms, she stood up to face her and said, "Listen to me. The vampires have organized themselves. It's not safe at night."

"It's never safe at night."

"It's even worse. Don't go out tonight especially. I'll search for Damien and Phoebe, but you and the others have to stay indoors. Okay?"

Mamá nodded. "Thank you, Gertoula. Please be careful. I fear for your safety, too. You are another of my babies, you know."

Gertie smiled as more tears streamed down her cheeks. Her throat tightened. She couldn't speak.

"Your mother is here in Athens. Did you know that?"

Gertie nodded. "Yes." She wanted to add, *and I'm looking right at her*, but she didn't. Instead, she said, "I'll come back with news as soon as possible."

After flying up the basement stairs, Gertie whisked out the front door and up into the foggy sky. She reached her mind out to Jeno, to Vladimir, and to the rest of their clan. Surprisingly she sensed them just a few miles away. Terrified but resolved, she followed their scents to the south.

Jeno's mind was guarded, so she was unable to get through to him until she was less than a mile away. He must have sensed her, for he reached out to her.

Gertie! It's not safe!

She came to a halt and hung in the foggy air, full of indecision. Before she could make up her mind over what to do, she was surrounded by members of Vladimir's clan.

With shocking speed, Vladimir flew to her and halted less than two feet away from her. "Welcome back. It's your turn to hold the baby."

Damien was thrust into her arms. He hissed at her and struggled to be free, but she held him tightly. "Please, Damien. It's okay. I'm your friend."

His mind was full of fear and hate.

"I wouldn't trust her, if I were you," Vladimir said. "I once thought she was my friend too. In fact, I had begun to love her like a daughter."

Vladimir spit at her and turned away.

"I want Bábá!" Damien cried.

She couldn't believe Vladimir would spit on her. She was still reeling from the shock when Jeno appeared before her.

"Where's Phoebe?" Gertie asked.

To her surprise and horror, Jeno stretched out his hand, and out of the fog appeared Nikita and Klaus's little sister. She had been turned into a vampire.

"What?" Gertie covered her mouth, reading the fear and despair in Phoebe's young mind. "How could you let this happen?" she asked Jeno.

"My father went to rescue Damien," Jeno said. "He felt sorry for him, buried alive in the tomb, just as he had been."

"But what about Phoebe? Why is she…?"

"Damien slipped from my father's arms. Baby vampires are the most dangerous and least predictable, and…."

"Oh no," Daphne cried.

"Damien went directly to Phoebe and drained her. She would have died if my father hadn't given her blood."

"I want Sissy," Damien said.

"Oh, no," Daphne repeated.

I'm scared, Phoebe said directly to Gertie's mind.

Phoebe? Gertie replied telepathically. *I promise to take care of you. Don't be scared.*

Gertie wished she could do something—anything—to make the little girl feel better.

"I want my Bábá," Damien said, struggling against Gertie's hold.

"We move on!" Vladimir shouted from the front of the ranks. "Bring the prisoners!"

That's when Gertie noticed the struggling demigod bound and held by four vampires. At first, she mistook the boy for Hector, but as she read his mind, she learned his name was Timothy. Gertie asked him telepathically if he knew where Hector was. The boy looked at her and shook his head.

Vladimir noticed the exchange and narrowed his eyes at Gertie.

Jeno gave Gertie a desperate look. *Get away from us as fast as you can. I'll distract the others somehow. Go!*

Even if she could escape with Damien, how could she leave Phoebe behind?

I can't.

A fellow clansman curled his hand around Gertie's free arm and said, "Let's go."

Jeno moved in and asserted himself between the other vampire and Gertie. "I'll take her from here."

Damien hissed in her arms.

"Please, Damien. It's all right. Jeno won't hurt you."

"It's not me he's afraid of," Jeno said as they took off toward the sea. "It's you."

"Why would he be afraid of me?" she asked.

"Vampire killer," Damien said in his little toddler voice.

Gertie's mouth dropped open. She glanced at Phoebe on one side of her and Jeno on the other before turning back to the little boy struggling in her arms. "Why would you say that to me?"

"Those were my father's words," Jeno said.

Gertie jerked up her chin. "I've never killed a vampire."

"Maybe not intentionally," Jeno said. "But by warning the demigods about our plan, well, we lost a lot of our people tonight."

Gertie didn't know what to say. She stared down at the sea below them and swallowed hard. "How many?"

"Two whole clans were annihilated, and the surviving clans lost at least one or two vampires each. Maybe a hundred total."

Faltering in the air, Gertie struggled to breathe. A balloon burst in her chest. As soon as she could speak, she asked, "How is that possible?"

"Homer was destroyed."

Gertie covered her mouth. "And he was the maker of…"

"Maybe thirty. But they were also makers."

"None reverted back to their human form? None of his clan survived?"

"He obeyed the laws against turning vampires. The members of his clan were all ancient bodies that disintegrated as soon as he was killed."

"Vampire killer," Damien said again.

"Please stop saying that," Gertie insisted. "You're frightening your sister."

Will I ever be human again? Phoebe asked her telepathically.

It dawned on Gertie that the only way to save Phoebe was to destroy Damien. How could she keep her promise to Mamá to save both of her babies? Tears pricked her eyes. She thought she would be sick, but she fought the overwhelming feelings of doom to be strong for Phoebe.

I will think of something, Phoeboula, Gertie replied. *Don't you worry, koureetsi mou.*

Phoebe turned her big brown eyes to Gertie and gave her the faintest smile.

That's when Gertie noticed that they had passed Alexander. She turned to Jeno. "Where are we going?"

"To the Minotaur's Labyrinth," Jeno said. *It's not too late to run away,* he added.

I told you. I can't. Why are you looking at me like that, Jeno?

I'm afraid for your life, he said, squeezing her arm. *I think my father intends to execute you.*

CHAPTER ELEVEN

The Mermaid and the Cave

Gertie blinked in disbelief. *But I can't leave Phoebe and Damien behind. I promised Mamá.*

Then grab Phoebe's arm and follow my lead.

Jeno took Gertie's hand, and they all four plummeted toward the water at the speed of light. Jeno dragged them down deep, toward the ocean floor, winding this way and that. Gertie lost her sense of direction and wasn't sure where they were in relation to the mainland. Just when Gertie thought she couldn't hold her breath any longer, they swam up to the surface and found themselves in an enormous, dark cave.

All four vampires sat on the rocky bank of the water and caught at the air.

"If they don't show up right on our heels, then we should be safe here," Jeno said.

They clustered close together, all eyes on the water. Gertie thought of the trash compactor scene in *A New Hope,* when Luke Skywalker and friends know the monster is lurking in the oozy garbage they're standing in.

"I want my Babá," Damien said.

Gertie held onto the little vampire, patting his back and rocking him back and forth as she stared anxiously at the sea.

Tears flooded Phoebe's eyes and streamed down her cheeks.

Gertie wiped them with one of her thumbs and said, "It's all going to be okay. You'll see."

Phoebe's tears turned to sobs. "I want to go home."

Gertie's eyes widened. She and Jeno exchanged grins.

"Phoebe! You can talk!"

Phoebe looked just as surprised as they, smiling through her tears. She pointed at her brother. "He let me go."

"What do you mean?" Gertie asked.

"Now that he's free, he let me go. He stopped possessing my mind."

Gertie adjusted Damien in her lap so that she could study his face. He had such a sweet little face with round brown eyes and dark wavy hair. He looked more like Nikita than any of the others, and this made Gertie smile and hug him. "I don't think he meant to possess your mind. I don't think he understands what's happening to him."

Phoebe pursed her lips and shook her head. "All he cares about is being free, nothing else."

"I don't think they're coming," Jeno said. "That means you have a fighting chance. And this cave is a perfect hideout. Better than I imagined."

"You've never been here before?" Gertie asked.

"No. I had no idea where I was going. I'm not even sure where we are, but I'll figure it out."

Gertie put an arm around Phoebe and said to Jeno, "Must have been hard for you to go against your father."

Jeno frowned. "He gave me no choice. I couldn't let him kill you."

"I want my Babá," Damien said again. "I'm hungry."

"We're all hungry." Gertie appealed to Jeno. "What should we do?"

"I'll go scout for a place to hide for the day, and then we'll feed at night."

"Don't leave us," Phoebe said, her face scrunched up again in tears. "I'm so scared."

"But you'll be safe here." He patted Phoebe on the back. "If the others didn't see where we went, they won't be able to track us. Vampires can't hear or smell underwater."

"Thank you for that interesting education in the ways of vampires," a female voice said from across the cave.

Jeno climbed to his feet and asked, "Who's there?"

The beautiful face of a woman emerged from the water. She watched them carefully as she swam to a rock and pulled herself out and onto it. She had the tail of a fish.

"A mermaid!" Phoebe cried and happily clapped her hands.

Gertie blinked her eyes and gawked.

"Who are you running from?" The mermaid pulled her wavy brown hair over one shoulder and combed it with her fingers.

"It doesn't matter," Jeno said. "They aren't coming."

She flapped her tail against the rock, changing positions. "What makes you so sure?"

"They'd be here by now."

She adjusted the seashell crown on her head. "How long do you expect to hideout here, in my cave."

"*Your* cave?" Gertie asked.

"Just until we find another place," Jeno said.

"You'd be a lot more comfortable in my husband's palace at the bottom of the sea."

"Wait," Gertie said with a big smile on her face. "I know who you are. You're Amphitrite, Poseidon's wife. I've read about you. You're a mermaid, you're beautiful, you wear a seashell crown, and your husband has a palace at the bottom of the sea. I can't believe I'm meeting Amphitrite." She turned to Jeno. "She's actually a Titaness—older than the Olympians, though you can't tell by looking at her. She doesn't age."

The mermaid smiled. "Thank you. As I said, I can take you to my husband's palace, if you wish. But I wouldn't recommend that you stay here in this cave much longer."

"Why?" Gertie asked.

Suddenly, a gigantic monster reared up from the water just behind the mermaid's rock. The monster's six necks were twice as long as the

Hydra's one, and its six serpent-like heads each had three rows of teeth and a darting, hissing tongue. It also had twelve long dangling legs, like tentacles, and the heads of six yelping dogs at its waist. Two long arms with pincers shot up from the monster's sides as it roared. Gertie had read about this monster and had recognized it immediately.

Scylla.

The mermaid on the rock didn't flinch but winked and whispered, "Coming?" just before she dove into the sea.

Jeno grabbed Gertie's hand, and Gertie took Phoebe's and held onto Damien as Jeno dragged them once again through the ocean on the heels of the goddess.

As they wound around coral and dodged schools of fish, Jeno said to her telepathically, *Just hold on. I'll get us to safety soon.*

It was weird hearing his thoughts in her mind but not hearing anything else in the whole wide sea. She realized Jeno had been right: vampires cannot hear or smell in water. She hadn't really noticed before because they had done all of their communicating underwater telepathically.

Now that they were far away from Scylla, Gertie relaxed a bit to enjoy the scenery. Light filtered in from the surface, adding vibrant color to everything. And it was breathtaking—the colorful schools of fish, the coral and anemone on the ocean floor, and the interesting shells of the crustaceans hobbling along below them.

The light also meant dawn had come. Gertie hoped they could stay at Poseidon's castle until dusk. She didn't want Phoebe and Damien to experience the scorching pain from the sun. She tried not to worry and focused, instead, on the exciting possibility that she would soon meet Poseidon, one of the most amazing gods in the pantheon.

As they came upon a steep drop in the ocean floor, the castle in the distance came into view. It wasn't what Gertie had expected. It looked more like a ruin than a lived-in castle and was covered in barnacles and seaweed. In books, the castle always appeared majestic and beautiful. Well, she supposed the stories didn't always get everything right.

A drawbridge opened and they followed the goddess inside. Unlike the vampires, Amphitrite could breathe and speak underwater, and she said something to the guards, but Gertie couldn't hear what. When she tried to read the goddess's mind, she found a powerful wall blocking it.

The guards escorted them into an antechamber that was empty of water. The pressure felt strange, and the air was dense and humid, making it less comfortable than the air above water.

"You can have a seat if you'd like." The mermaid pointed at a bed of smooth boulders on one side of the room.

Gertie held Damien in her arms and sat between Phoebe and Jeno on the black rocks. Across from them was an object that resembled a scale. On the bottom was a silver square platform, and above it was a gauge with a red needle. On the left, in green letters, the gauge read, "kalós," the Greek word for "good." On the right, in red letters, it read, "kakós," the Greek word for "bad."

Amphitrite noticed them studying it. She glided on her tail over to it and said, "This was once Apollo's. It's a magical scale that tells me which of my guests is good and which is bad. The good guests get my husband's assistance; but the bad ones are fed to our children."

Gertie's throat tightened.

"Fed to your children?" Jeno asked, squeezing Gertie's hand.

"You should have nothing to fear. From your conversation in the cave, it sounds as though you are all good people, even if you *are* vampires."

But Gertie did have something to fear. She wasn't sure if any of them were completely good, especially her.

"Who are your children?" Gertie asked.

"You met one of them in the cave," the mermaid said with a wry grin.

Oh, no! Gertie said to Jeno. *I think I was wrong.*

Yeah, I figured that out, too.

"Your husband isn't Poseidon, is it?" Gertie asked in a quavering voice.

The mermaid shook her head. "His name is Phorcys."

"I know who you are." Gertie swallowed hard. Her throat was tight and felt like it had a lump in it.

"Oh?" the mermaid taunted.

"Keto," Gertie said. "The mother of monsters."

"I'm glad we got that straightened out," Keto said. "I didn't want to correct you before and appear rude. Who would like to climb onto the scale first?"

"That's okay," Jeno said. "Thank you anyway. We'll be on our way."

"I'm afraid that's not possible," Keto said. "The only way I can let you leave is if you have a pure heart. If your heart isn't pure, well, then, it would be wrong to let you go."

Gertie tightened her hold on Damien as Phoebe's eyes filled with tears.

"Then I'll go first." Jeno climbed onto the silver platform.

Gertie was afraid to look at the gauge. Sweat beaded on her forehead. She hugged Damien close and squeezed Phoebe's hand. She was shocked and relieved when the needle swung to the "good" side.

"Now the little girl," Keto demanded.

Trembling, Phoebe stepped to the platform.

Gertie held her breath but wasn't surprised when the needle swung to the "good" side.

"All right, then," the goddess said. "See? I said you have nothing to fear."

"I'll go next," Gertie said, handing Damien over to Phoebe.

Her legs were shaking uncontrollably as she stepped onto the silver platform. Unable to see the gauge herself, she was terrified when Jeno frowned.

"I'm bad?" Gertie asked. "I don't have a pure heart?"

"Not bad and not good," Keto said. "The needle stayed right in the middle."

"What does that mean?" Gertie asked through chattering teeth.

"It means your destiny is still undecided," Keto said. "You could go either way."

"So you won't feed me to your children?" Gertie asked.

Keto pulled her brown hair over one shoulder and began combing it with her fingers. "I don't think I can risk letting you go. What if you end up a villain?"

Gertie ran to Jeno's arms. *What can we do? Don't let her feed me to the monsters!*

"I need the baby to get on the scale." Keto slid over to Phoebe and pried Damien from her arms. "Stand here, little boy."

"I want my Babá!" Damien cried, breaking into sobs.

Keto stepped back from the scale and all of them looked up at the gauge. To Gertie's horror, the needle swung fully over to the "bad" side.

"Oh, dear," Keto said, smiling.

Just then, the door to the antechamber burst open, and a legion of vampires swarmed inside, flying in all directions as the water spilled in and began filling up the room.

Before Damien was overtaken by the flood, he said with glee, "Babá! You came!"

C H A P T E R   T W E L V E

Death Sentence

Gertie woke up in darkness, slouched against a wall of rock. Someone sat close beside her—too close for her to get a look at the person's face. Before she could reach out with her mind to figure out who it was, the person spoke.

"You're awake?"

"Hector?" She couldn't believe it. "Hector, is it really you?"

"Yes. Are you hurt?"

"Where's Phoebe? Where's Damien?"

"What do you mean? Why would you ask me about Phoebe and Damien?"

She explained to him what had happened.

"I can't believe this! Man, I just can't." He jumped up and paced the chamber. "Are they hurt?"

"I don't know. I don't know where they are. I can't sense them anymore."

Hector balled his fists. "I'm going to kill those tramps."

"Please don't talk like that. What happened to you, anyway?"

He took a deep breath and let it out. "I went back to my father's temple last night. I prayed to him, but he didn't appear. I tried to tell him what you said, about vampires being people, about appealing to the other gods for help. On my way back home, I was captured and brought here."

"I'm so sorry. Did they get anyone else?"

"I don't know."

"They didn't hurt you, did they?"

He shook his head. "What about you? Are you hurt?"

"I'm fine." She was exhausted and starving, but nothing felt broken. If she'd been injured in the battle at Keto and Phorcyth's castle, she had already healed. "I'm glad you're okay. I was worried they'd killed you."

"I was better before you got here."

She blanched. "How can you say that to me?"

"I thought maybe Jeno would protect you, keep you from this place. You here? Not good."

"Oh. What is this place?"

"The Minotaur's labyrinth."

That was good news to her. "Asterion and Ariadne are my friends. Maybe they could…"

"No. They can't. Dionysus controls them."

"How?"

"He's got something over them. I don't know. All that matters is that we're at his mercy."

"What are they planning to do with us?" she asked.

He didn't need to answer. She could read his mind.

"We've got to get out of here." He pointed to the wooden door. "We'll have to ambush the next person that comes through. Kill them, if possible. Think you can handle that?"

She wasn't sure. "Kill them?"

"It's either them or us now, Gertie. Do you get that? It's them or us."

She let that sink in and then nodded. "Okay." She wasn't sure if she could really do it, but she wanted to believe she could. "I'll help you kill the next person who comes through that door."

"I think we'll have a better chance if you bite me."

She wrinkled her brow. "Only if the person comes in the next six hours."

"What if you keep biting me? Don't drink, just bite?"

She licked her lips without thinking.

He blushed.

"I'm so sorry." She turned white. "I'm just so hungry. I'm starving."

"Then drink, Gertie. My God, please." He cupped her face. "Seriously, do it."

Her fangs extended of their own accord, and the shock in Hector's eyes didn't even deter her as she pressed them into his neck. He stroked her hair as she drew in the warm nourishment. When she had taken a half a pint, she stopped herself.

Hector held onto her as the dizzy ecstasy took over.

"Thank you," she said. "You're so kind. So selfless. I'm not."

When he could speak, he said, "You are. I've seen it."

"During the fall dance, I was trying to help, trying to figure out what had gotten into Phoebe. She'd stopped signing, you know?"

He nodded.

"Then when everything went all crazy, after I got kicked out and you took me in, I tried to go back to erase their minds, hoping for a fresh start."

He pushed a strand of her hair out of her face and said, "I know."

"That was selfish of me. None of this would be happening right now if…" she dropped off, crossing her arms, her throat too tight with regret to continue. She couldn't stop the tears from coming. They poured down her cheeks as she cried over what she had done. All of this was her fault.

Hector put his arms around her and held her close, resting his chin on the top of her head.

"None of this is your fault," he whispered. "This was building up long before either of us was born."

"Why didn't I listen to you and stay away from the vampires?"

"Maybe this is all part of a greater plan."

They both sensed a presence at the door and heard a chink of keys in the padlock. Like a gust of wind, they lifted off the ground and flattened their backs against the ceiling of the cave, just above the door. The plan was to spring on whoever opened the door, spring to kill, and then make a run for it. Gertie's heart hammered in her chest as she tried to get a reading on the person at the door.

Just as the door cracked open, she sensed who it was.

Wait! she shouted into Hector's mind. *It's Phoebe!*

Phoebe lifted her face toward them, her mouth wide open in surprise.

"Phoebe!" Hector moved to the ground beside her and hugged her. "Are you okay?"

"It was smart of them to send her," Gertie said. "Very smart."

"They're right outside," Phoebe said.

Hector stepped back and gawked. "You can talk?"

The little girl blushed and nodded.

Hector hugged Phoebe once more. Gertie sensed that he was too choked up to speak. She flew down beside them, and, together, they opened the door all the way and peered outside their chamber.

A legion of vampires was lined up all along the narrow corridor.

"Where's Damien?" Hector whispered.

"On Vladimir's back," Phoebe said. "Just like a little backpack."

Gertie and Hector exchanged looks of concern as Phoebe led them from the room.

"This way," she said. "Vladimir is waiting for us."

Hector took Gertie's hand, and they followed Phoebe past the line of vampire guards. The tunnel eventually forked. They took the corridor to the right. Gertie searched for Jeno among the faces and reached out with her mind, but she could not find him. When the tunnel opened up into a much larger chamber, Gertie realized why she hadn't seen Jeno. He was bound by chains to the stone wall. Was he to be executed, too? Would Vladimir kill his own son?

Jeno, are you okay? She reached out to his mind, but it was blocked, and he did not answer.

Across the room, with Damien on his back, stood Vladimir. He instructed two vampire guards to chain Gertie and Hector to the wall alongside Jeno. Gertie's knees were so weak with fear that she found it easier to fly a few inches from the ground than to walk.

One of the vampires forced her back against the wall as the other chained her. A very large vampire stood in the center of the room holding a very heavy ax.

A beheading. This was the way she and her friends would die.

I don't want to die, she said to all who might be listening. *I didn't mean for Homer and the others to get killed.*

Phoebe was sobbing now, but Gertie refused to cry. She didn't want to spend the last few moments of her life in tears.

Vladimir stepped toward the middle of the room and said, "My brothers and sisters, today we mourn the deaths of ninety-eight of our friends and family members, our fallen champions of the uprising." He took a scroll from the inside of his cloak, opened it, and then read the names of every person who had died, starting with Homer. "Aesop, Agatha, Bartholomew, Bernice…." When he had finished, he said, "It's important to remember that each of these warriors were people just like you and me, hoping for a better future. Most of the gods and humans don't see that. They think of us as creatures rather than people; but we are people, and we demand justice."

As the vampires in the cavern applauded, Gertie was overwhelmed by the thought that all those lives were on her conscience. She had been responsible for their deaths.

No. Hector said in her mind. *The vampires were responsible for those deaths. They were the ones who decided to attack humans. You did the right thing.*

Vladimir silenced the crowd. "History has shown us that if a civilization is in need of change, a monumental effort must be made, and that effort usually involves brute force, violence, and sacrifice." Vladimir stepped closer to Hector. "Injustice never fixes itself. No one in power willingly gives up his power. If people are subjugated, they must take the power for themselves."

Several of the vampires shouted words of approval.

"It's unfortunate, but necessary," Vladimir said. "Gertrude's act of betrayal has sent the message to our enemies that we are weak and divided and that our cause is not to be taken seriously."

The crowd moaned a horrific "boo" to express its disapproval.

Gertie's knees nearly buckled beneath her. She hovered when she couldn't stand.

Vladimir lifted his hand for silence and said, "I took her in as my own daughter, and she betrayed me. She betrayed *us*. Nearly one hundred lives were lost, and our efforts have been severely thwarted. For this, Gertrude Morgan must die."

A roar of applause exploded in the cavern, echoing and ringing in Gertie's ears. She had to struggle not to vomit.

The axman raised his ax in the air as a way of cheering on the crowd.

She turned to Jeno and said, "I love you, and I'm so sorry."

It is I who am sorry, Jeno said telepathically.

She gave him a sad smile. Then she turned to Hector and said, "And I love you, too, Hector. Oh, Hector..." Her sobs overtook her, and she couldn't speak.

Hector looked at her with sad and frightened eyes. "Pray to my father to save us."

Instead, she prayed to the god she believed was her own—Dionysus.

Save your daughter and her friends. If Hector dies, so will this uprising. If you spare us, we can help you back. We can steal something from the Olympians to get their attention. Show us that you really care about your children and the children of the night.

Her teeth were shattering, but she was beginning to feel numb and surprisingly calm. It was like the time the dentist had used laughing gas on her. Everything had seemed so surreal. That's how this felt, like she was floating outside of her body and it was all a dream.

Then, when the axman stepped forward, something clicked in her mind, and she turned to Vladimir and shouted, "You would kill your own son? Why are you fighting this war, if not for him?"

"I'm not going to kill him," Vladimir sneered. "His punishment is to watch."

"I'd rather you kill me," Jeno said. "I've never been more ashamed to be a vampire."

"Let's get this over with," Vladimir muttered.

The axman positioned himself right in front of Gertie. He lifted the heavy ax up in the air. Gertie closed her eyes and said goodbye to the world. Several more seconds went by and nothing happened. When she opened her eyes again, she saw a wall of thick, golden vines surrounding her, Jeno, and Hector. They grew between them and everyone else, reminding her of the dream she had had the night of the dance with the Maenads and satyrs.

"What's happening?" She looked back and forth at her two friends, but they were as shocked as she was. "What's going on?"

"It appears that our lord, Dionysus, does not want you killed," Vladimir said angrily on the other side of the vines.

"I wonder why?" the axman muttered.

Gertie finally allowed the tears that had been pricking her eyes to fall down her face as relief swept over her. She had really thought it was going to be the end.

The golden vines twisted and turned and began to recede back down into the rocky ground, but something white was left behind in their place. It was flat, like a platter, but had something written on it. Vladimir commanded the nearest vampire to pick it up and bring it to him.

"It's Persephone's platter," Vladimir said. "At least, it has her name, along with 'Queen of the Underworld,' inscribed on it. I wonder why Dionysus has left this for me."

Suddenly a bunch of red, ripe grapes appeared on the platter.

"The grapes from the vine of our lord," Vladimir said.

Gertie doubted it would prove to be enough leverage for negotiating for the vampires' freedom. How much would they care about one goddess's platter, even if it was magical?

Then inspiration struck her like a bolt of lightning. It was a gift.

"Dionysus wants us to deliver it to Persephone as a gift," Gertie said. "Because he wants us to steal something while we're there."

"Steal something?" Vladimir repeated.

"What's the most powerful thing in the Underworld?" she asked.

"Lord Hades," Vladimir said.

"The most powerful object," she clarified.

Vladimir stepped closer to her and studied her. "Our lord wants you to steal the helm of invisibility?"

"He wants *us* to steal it," she said.

"Us?" Vladimir asked.

"Me and Hector. I need a wing man."

"Why not Jeno?" Vladimir suggested. "Someone I can trust?"

"We need someone Hades can trust," she said. "Someone who isn't a vampire."

"Yes, I see," Vladimir said. "So the helm will become our leverage."

"That's right." Gertie smiled triumphantly. "Not human beings, but something better."

"Jeno will go with you, too," Vladimir insisted.

Gertie glanced first at Jeno and then at Hector, trying to read their minds. Jeno's was heavily guarded, but Hector's was clear:

We may have survived the vampires, but if we steal the helm, Hades will kill us for sure.

CHAPTER THIRTEEN

The Underworld

At nightfall, Gertie and Jeno each held one of Hector's arms as they set off from the labyrinth at Knossos and flew over the sea for Athens. Jeno knew of only one way into the Underworld, and it was beneath a mound of rubble at the acropolis.

"Over there," he said, pointing.

They landed beneath the moonlight next to a construction site where the humans had already begun work on reconstructing the mess Athena had made.

"Dig here," Jeno said, laying down the pack that held Persephone's platter. "Until we find the sinkhole."

"What if we don't get through before daybreak?" Gertie asked, not looking forward to being scorched by the sun.

"We dig fast," Jeno said. "I don't know of any other way."

They all three began pulling stones from the heap and tossing them into the back of a huge truck, where the humans had already dumped a good amount of rubble.

"What's our plan?" Hector asked. "We go inside with the platter and say we have this gift from Dionysus. Then what?"

Jeno shook his head. "They're going to thank us and tell us to leave, so we need to delay that somehow."

"Do we even know where the helm is kept?" Gertie asked.

"In Hades's private chambers," Jeno said.

"Impossible to get to." Hector hefted up a large stone and tossed it angrily into the back of the truck. "This mission is impossible."

"No, it's not," Gertie said, as she, too, flung rocks onto the pile. "We just have to think."

"We have invisibility," Jeno said. "The two of you can distract Hades and Persephone with the gift. Keep them occupied for as long as you can while I steal the helm."

"But Hades doesn't know either one of us," Gertie said to Jeno. "*You* should be presenting the gift. After all, it's from the lord of the vampires. It should come from a vampire."

"*You* are a vampire," Jeno said.

Hector's mouth pressed into a thin line.

"You and Hector present the platter," she said to Jeno. "Otherwise, they'll wonder how we got inside. If they see you, they'll know."

"How?" Hector asked.

"He's been going there for centuries to groom Hades's horses."

Hector lifted his brows. "Good to know. Maybe this mission isn't so impossible."

"So, we're good then?" she asked. "I'm stealing the helm."

"I should steal it," Hector said. "Hades is less likely to kill me if I get caught, since I'm the son of Hephaestus and grandson of Apollo."

Gertie frowned. "I'd have to bite you again."

"So?" Hector lifted his hands in the air.

Jeno shook his head. "It would take too long to teach you how to use invisibility."

"I'm a fast learner," Hector insisted. "Let me do this."

Gertie turned to Jeno. "We *have* been seen together in the Underworld once before."

Jeno sighed. "I don't know."

"It's the only plan that makes sense," Hector said.

After a beat, Jeno said, "Okay, but we need to dig faster."

"Gertie should bite me." Hector stood up and clinched his fists. "That way I can practice invisibility."

"Once I bite you, you'll only have about five or six hours before the power wears off."

"I need to practice," Hector repeated. "Come on."

Gertie glanced at Jeno, who nodded. Then she stood up and took Hector's wrist, since the wound on his neck was still healing. Before she put her teeth to his flesh, she noticed his hand trembling.

"You don't have to be afraid," she whispered, feeling like a monster.

"I'm not afraid."

She looked into his mind and discovered the real reason he was trembling. It was her touch. Her touch made him excited and nervous and charged with energy. She blushed with a mixture of relief and confusion and closed her eyes as she sank her fangs into his wrist.

After she had taken several draws, Jeno said, "That's enough. Stop, in case he needs to be bitten again later."

Gertie nodded and wiped her mouth. "Sorry."

Hector's eyes were closed. He was momentarily paralyzed. Gertie was still in his head, experiencing the ecstasy of the vampire bite right along with him. That, along with the strength that came with feeding, bolstered her stamina and mood. She sighed and went back to digging, and in a few moments, Hector did, too.

As they picked up the pace, Jeno and Gertie explained to Hector how to achieve invisibility. Occasionally, Hector would stop digging to practice. Once he got the hang of it, Jeno suggested that Hector remain invisible until they found the sinkhole.

"I'll try not to take that personally," Hector said with a laugh.

"When should he strip down?" Gertie asked.

"When should I *what?*" Hector asked.

"Didn't you notice that we can still see your clothes when you go invisible?" Gertie pointed out.

"I thought it was just me seeing them."

"He should do it after we get by the Hydra," Jeno said. "He can hide his clothes and sword in the stables."

It felt like a miracle when, an hour later, after the truck was already full, Gertie came upon stones that were wet. The discovery rejuvenated the three of them, and they dug faster. Soon they had cleared the sinkhole to find a body of water about ten feet in diameter.

"This should lead to the Hydra's hole," Jeno said. "Are we ready?"

Hector let out the energy he'd been holding, in order to become visible to them again. "Ready."

Gertie took a deep breath and, as she exhaled, said, "Ready."

"The Hydra will not be happy to see us," Jeno said to Hector. "Just follow my lead, and as soon as we get to the other side, fly to the top of the cavern, flat against the ceiling. Got it?"

"Got it," Hector said.

Jeno dove in, wearing the backpack with Persephone's platter. Gertie followed. Hector took up the rear.

As soon as they emerged on the other side, the Hydra screamed and lunged for them. Gertie and Jeno flattened against the ceiling in a flash, but Hector drew his sword.

Gertie had forgotten how enormous and terrifying the Hydra was with her dragon head, sharp teeth, and flaming breath. The monster shrieked and snapped as the eight headless necks flapped wildly. Hector ducked and swung around to the back of her. She reared up, turned, and lunged again, this time singeing the ends of his wet blond hair. He swung at her with his sword, missed, and leaped out of the way as flames shot from her mouth.

"Stop!" Jeno shouted.

Hector tried to listen to Jeno, tried to lift up toward the ceiling, but the Hydra pierced his jeans with a claw and had him hooked, like live bait on the end of a fishing string.

"Hector!" Gertie squealed, flying toward him.

Jeno grabbed her arm and pulled her back just as the Hydra's tail swept around toward Gertie. It would have crushed her had Jeno not acted. Hector twisted his body around and came down hard with his sword right across the Hydra's claw, freeing himself and trimming her nails simultaneously.

Gertie smiled with relief as Hector flew toward them, but her smile was premature. The Hydra reached out with her other claws and snatched Hector away. As the monster was about to fry him with her flaming breath, Hector sliced free of her grip. She grabbed at him again with bleeding claws. He jumped up, turned around with his sword flying, and then swung the blade right across her neck. The Hydra's head fell into the pool of water with a loud splash.

"No!" Jeno shouted. "She was just doing her job!"

"She tried to kill me!" Hector yelled back.

"Why did you draw your sword in the first place?" Jeno asked.

Hector's face turned red. "Instinct."

Gertie put a hand on Jeno's shoulder. "She's immortal, right? Hector didn't kill her."

"We need to get out of here," Jeno said. "Follow me."

When they reached the stables, the Fury Megaera appeared to them with her falcon perched on her shoulder.

"What are you doing here, Jeno?" she asked. "I told you not to come back."

"My lord, Dionysus, asked me and my friends to bring Lady Persephone a gift."

"A gift?" she repeated.

Jeno removed his backpack and took out the platter. He handed it to Megaera, whose eyes lit up with surprise when the beautiful grapes appeared.

"The grapes are from the vines of Dionysus," Jeno said.

"How do we know they aren't poisoned?" she asked.

Hector reached over and plucked one before popping it into his mouth. "Delicious."

"Why would Dionysus give this to my mother?" the Fury asked.

Jeno hesitated.

"Because we have a favor to ask in return," Gertie said quickly.

Megaera arched a brow. "What favor?"

"We aren't at liberty to tell you," Hector said. "It's for your father and mother's ears, and no one else's."

"Very well, but I'll be watching you." She handed over the platter to Jeno and vanished.

Great. I've been seen. Hector said to them telepathically. *So much for using invisibility.*

Gertie, what were you thinking? What favor are we going to ask? Jeno's thoughts assaulted her as he stuffed the now empty platter back into his pack.

I don't know. Gertie admitted. *The Fury wanted a reason. That was the first thing that came to mind.*

We can ask to speak with Tiresias. Hector said. *That's our favor. To ask him how the uprising will turn out.*

Oh, that's brilliant! Gertie said. *Don't you think so, Jeno?*

Not brilliant, but it will do. Hector, take off your clothes and leave them and your sword here, in the stables.

But I've been seen, Hector objected. *That Fury already knows I'm here.*

We don't know that she's told anyone yet, Jeno said. *We've got to stick with the plan, unless you got a better idea?*

Hector went invisible and did as Jeno said.

I'm not too keen on leaving my sword behind, Hector said as he strapped the belt to Gertie's waist. *You wear it. Just in case.*

Jeno led them past the stables, following the river of fire, until they came upon a huge iron door.

"Meet us back at the acropolis," Jeno whispered.

"Fine," Hector said. "If you get caught, pray for mercy."

"Hades isn't well-known for his mercy." Jeno knocked on the door.

A beautiful goddess with long black hair streaked with white opened the door and asked, "What's this? How did you get past Cerberus?"

A Doberman growled through the opening.

"Is that Cubie?" Gertie whispered in disbelief.

The Doberman grew quiet as the goddess asked, "How do you know my Cubie?"

"I've read about her," Gertie said. "She used to be the queen of Troy. You must be Hecate, Persephone's, like, best friend. Is Galin here, too?"

"Who are you and how did you get past the gate?" the goddess demanded.

Jeno stepped forward. "We came by way of the Hydra. I'm Jeno, the vampire who has served Lord Hades for centuries as a groomsman."

"What are you doing here?" she asked.

"Dionysus has asked me and my friend to present a magical gift to Lady Persephone."

"Let them in, Hecate," a deep voice boomed from inside. "I know why they're here."

"As you wish, Lord Hades." Hecate opened the door and stepped aside.

Gertie and Jeno exchanged looks of concern before entering. When Hecate slammed the iron door shut behind them, Gertie feared Hector hadn't had enough time to get through.

Are you with us, Hector?

He didn't answer.

Hades towered above them, beautiful and magnificent, with curly black hair and steely black eyes. Beside him stood someone whom Gertie supposed was his equally beautiful wife. Her long hair, the color of corn, was adorned with a pomegranate flower just behind her ear.

Gertie and Jeno stood side by side looking up at the king and queen of the Underworld.

Hades crossed his arms and then reached up with one hand to pick at his beard. "So, you've come to steal my helm."

CHAPTER FOURTEEN

Hades

Gertie looked again at Jeno. *What do we do?*

I don't know. I guess we tell the truth. Jeno turned to Hades. *Here goes nothing.* "Yes. We came to take your helm."

Hecate moved beside Persephone. "So, it's true?"

"Smart." Persephone lifted her chin. "It's best not to contradict my husband."

"We also came to give you this gift." Gertie took the platter from Jeno and handed it to Persephone. "From Dionysus."

Bunches of grapes appeared on the platter, which brought a smile to the queen's face.

"Tell me why you want it." Hades narrowed his eyes.

Jeno opened his mouth to speak again but shut it.

Say something, Gertie pleaded.

"Take your time," Hades said. "Think carefully."

I can't rat out my own father, Jeno said telepathically.

"But not too much time," Hades warned. "I don't have all day."

Nothing good can come from anything I say, Jeno said in Gertie's mind.

Hades sighed impatiently.

"Here's the problem," Gertie blurted out. "The vampires can't get humans and gods to respect them. It's not fair, the way they're forced to live, mostly in poverty, looked down on by the rest of society. It's just not fair."

Hades picked at his beard again. "No one has ever said that life is fair."

"But it's the responsibility of humans and gods to try to make it as fair as possible," Gertie said.

Hades bent over and glared at Gertie, his nose inches from hers. "It's *not* the responsibility of humans to tell gods what to do."

"I'm not a human," she said quickly as the little bit of blood pumping through her veins rushed to her face. "I'm a vampire."

"So you are," Hades observed.

Jeno gave her a faint smile.

"A wise person once said that injustice never fixes itself," Gertie argued. "People have to act."

"Good point, little vampire," Hades said. "Good point, indeed."

Gertie and Jeno exchanged looks of surprise.

"You've shocked them, dear," Persephone said to her husband with a smile.

Gertie smiled, too. "I knew it."

"Knew what?" Hades arched a brow.

"I knew you were a just god," she said. "Different stories depict you differently. Some make you seem evil, like a demon; and others show you as just and fair. I had a feeling, and I was right."

"Don't draw conclusions too hastily," he said. "I've decided to help you, but I have some conditions."

"There's always a price," Gertie said. "I've read that, too."

Hades frowned, and Gertie could tell she was annoying him. She clamped her mouth closed and tried to hold back from saying anything else.

"First things first," he said. "Are you willing to turn over your little demigod friend, who's currently sneaking around my bed chamber?"

Gertie felt the blood leave her face. "What? Why? What would you do?" Her throat tightened.

"Execute him. Send him to Tartarus until his penalty was paid, especially after what he did to Hydra."

Gertie swallowed hard. "No. No we aren't willing to turn him over."

"And do you agree, Jeno?" Hades asked.

Jeno glanced at Gertie and then nodded. "I agree. He's our friend. We can't sacrifice him."

"Even for my help?" Hades asked.

Jeno nodded.

"You would give up the chance to liberate an entire race of people, just to spare one person's eternal damnation?"

What a mean trick, Jeno said telepathically to Gertie. *I can't believe he'd put us in this position.*

We can't betray Hector, Gertie replied.

Agreed. Out loud, Jeno said, "He helped us. We can't betray him."

"Hecate, fetch the demigod for me, please," Hades commanded.

Hecate vanished and returned within seconds with her hands firmly at Hector's wrists.

"He came here because he had no choice," Hades said. "He's here to save his own skin."

"That's not true," Gertie said without thinking.

"You contradict my husband?" Persephone glared at her.

Gertie felt herself trembling all over. This was so much worse than she had imagined. She could think of nothing to do but to drop to her knees and beg for mercy.

"Please don't kill Hector, Lord Hades," she pleaded. "We're sorry. We just needed leverage—something other than human lives."

"Human lives?" Hades asked.

Gertie told him about Vladimir's original plan.

"When Dionysus sent us the platter, we thought it meant he wanted us to come and..." Gertie dropped off.

"So it seems," Hades said.

"But Hector doesn't deserve to die," Jeno said. "We won't make the trade."

In that moment, Gertie knew she would always love Jeno.

Hades turned his back to them and took several steps across the room, where the Doberman sat beside a weasel. "I wasn't going to kill your demigod friend."

"You weren't?" Gertie studied the god's face.

"It was a test?" Jeno asked.

"And you passed it," Persephone pointed out. "Now we know you are loyal."

"But I still need to be sure you're worthy," Hades said, turning to face them again. "So I have a quest for you. There's something I need. If you can obtain this object for me, I will help you."

Hector dropped to his knees beside Gertie. "I'll do whatever you ask. Just name it, my lord."

Jeno went down on his knees on the other side of Gertie, so that they all three were now kneeling before the king and queen and their friend. "We are you servants."

Hades's eyes twinkled, and he picked at his beard. "Well then." He moved closer to the three and said, "I need you to steal Athena's shield and bring it to me."

He has to be joking, Hector thought, and Gertie agreed. Why would Hades ask such a thing?

Jeno opened his mouth and then shut it again. Gertie read the conflict in his mind. Finally, he said, "Would you mind telling us why you need it?"

"Does it matter?" Hades asked.

"Yes," Hector said. Then telepathically, he added, *I'm with you, brother. The "why" definitely matters.*

Gertie glanced at Hector and then at Jeno, realizing for the first time how alike they were. One might be a vampire and the other a demigod, but they were both noble and brave. No wonder she was in love with them.

Hector cleared his throat and blushed. He had heard her thoughts.

"We came here for the helm to give the vampires a way to negotiate for their freedom," Hector added. "We always intended to give it back. The 'why' matters, Lord Hades."

"But you just said you were my servants, that you'd do anything," Hades reminded them.

"They misspoke," Gertie said. "And we never expected you to ask us to steal something from Athena. We thought you were just."

"How dare you?" Persephone accused.

Gertie's face grew bright red.

Hades turned away to pace again. "It's interesting how many times you have made assumptions, little vampire. First, you assume I'm just. Then you assume I'm not. You base this on little, if any, evidence. Is this how you typically go through life? Making judgments based on assumptions?"

She supposed it *was* true, but she didn't want to admit it.

"Do any of you know why Medusa's head is on Athena's shield?" Hades asked.

"Perseus gave it to her," Gertie said. "At least, that's what the stories say. He was sent to slay Medusa by a king who wanted Perseus out of the way."

"But why give the head to Athena?" Hades asked.

"According to the stories, she's the one who turned Medusa into a monster," Gertie answered.

"And why would Athena do such a thing?" Persephone asked before she popped a grape into her mouth.

"Because Medusa had an affair with Poseidon in Athena's temple," Gertie said.

"An affair?" Hecate snapped. "Is that what the stories say?"

"Some say *raped*," Gertie admitted. "But I can't believe that of Poseidon."

"Believe it," Hades said.

"Maybe not raped," Persephone said. "But certainly seduced. Medusa was young and innocent. Poseidon took advantage of her, and yet *she* was punished for it."

Gertie didn't like to accept anything negative about her favorite gods. As a reader, she had chosen to believe the good parts about Poseidon and Athena and the others. She had chosen to ignore the bad parts. In fact, from what she'd read, something similar had happened to Persephone. Hadn't Hades abducted her?

"We all make mistakes," Hades said. "But Medusa has paid for hers beyond what she owed. I want to grant her immortality and a place in my kingdom. She may even prove to be a strong ally for the vampires."

Hector stood up. "What if you petition Athena…"

"Don't you think I've tried?" Hades interrupted.

But wasn't Athena a goddess of wisdom and justice? Wasn't she also an advocate for women? "Why would she be like that?" Gertie asked.

"It's a mystery," Hades said. "And if she won't return Medusa's head, we have no choice."

"So, we get your help at the price of Athena's vengeance?" Hector asked. "I'm not sure that's a good deal."

"Your vampire friends told you to return with the helm," Hades said. "What do you suppose will happen to you if you fail?"

Jeno climbed to his feet now, too. "So how do you propose we get Medusa's head?"

"If I knew that, I wouldn't need you," Hades said. "But if you want to borrow my helm, I need you to figure it out."

"We obviously can't get away with invisibility," said Hector. "Not if you saw me. It must not work on the gods."

"I didn't see you. I have wards of protection drawn all over this chamber, and they alerted me to your presence."

"Athena will have something similar, won't she?" Gertie asked, climbing to her feet, too.

"We need to draw her out," Jeno said. "Away from her temple."

"I'll leave the details to you," Hades said. "But I want you to know something. The vampires made a mistake when they made Dionysus their lord."

Gertie's eyes widened. That was her *father*. "What do you mean?"

"The god of the vine might be a champion for the underdog when he's sober, but that isn't often, now is it?" Hades said.

"You think it should be *you*?" Hector asked.

"Well, they *do* dwell in my caves," Hades said. "And they are also technically part of the dead."

"I'm not dead," Jeno said.

"You are the *living* dead," Hades said. "And you should belong to my flock."

"Are you asking the vampires to depose their lord?" Hector asked.

"No," the god of the Underworld began to pace again. "No, that wouldn't be good for anybody."

"Then what are you saying?" Jeno asked.

Hades turned and rushed across the room and pointed an angry finger at Jeno. "I'm saying you children of the night should remember what you are. You are the dead, and you belong to my kingdom. I'm saying you should stop fooling yourselves into thinking you can ever make it up there. You need to come home."

"But we need human blood," Jeno said.

"You don't think I can provide?" Hades challenged.

No one seemed to know what to say.

"Think about it." Hades turned away. "Now go to Charon for safe passage out of here, and don't return without Athena's shield."

CHAPTER FIFTEEN

Charon

Hecate opened the iron door, and Gertie followed Hector and Jeno through. Once it was closed behind them, they stood there, recovering. All three were shaken and not sure what to make of their encounter with the lord of the Underworld.

"Thank you," Hector said to them. "You saved my life."

"Hades said it was only a test," Jeno pointed out. "He wasn't going to kill you."

"Maybe," Hector said. "Or maybe he only said that after you refused."

"It was the right thing to do," Jeno said.

"Maybe," Hector shrugged. "Maybe not. But thank you."

Jeno smiled and shook his head.

"What's so funny?" Gertie asked.

"I never thought I'd see the day when a demigod would look me in the eyes and see me for what I really am—as something more than a vampire."

Hector smiled too. "Yeah, well, don't get too used to it."

They all three smiled at what they knew was a joke. Since Hector didn't know how to block his mind, it was an open book, just as Gertie's had been as a new vampire. Gertie sucked in her lips and quickly guarded her own thoughts after reading Hector's: *You're making it difficult for me to want to kill your father.*

The other day, Gertie had insisted to Hector that she didn't want to be "saved," but as the reality of her being a vampire *forever* sunk in, she felt overwhelmed by melancholy. She was a vampire, and she needed to get used to it.

Neither Jeno nor Gertie replied to Hector's joke. Instead, they turned and followed the Phlegethon where it met the River Styx and waited for Charon to appear, as they'd been instructed to do.

Finding a seat on a nearby rock on the bank of the Styx, Gertie wondered how on earth they would ever get to Athena's shield.

Gertie must have let down her guard, because, as Jeno sat beside her, he replied to her thoughts with, "I wonder, too."

Hector paced along the bank, reminding her of Hades. "Like you said, we'll have to lure Athena away from her temple. It's probably warded." Then he went up to Gertie and took his scabbard from her waist and fit it to his own. "Thanks for holding onto this. I'm still not wearing any clothes, am I?"

She blushed bright red and shook her head. "It wouldn't matter anyway. Jeno and I can see right through them."

"It would matter to me," he said. "I can't get used to this."

Gertie understood how he felt.

"We'll stop by your place on the way to the acropolis," Jeno said. "You can get more clothes then."

"Thanks," Hector said.

"Now, back to our plan," Jeno said. "How can we lure Athena from her temple?"

Hector continued to pace. "People are motivated by what they love and by what they hate, right?"

Gertie had never really thought about it, but she supposed Hector was right. "Makes sense."

"So what does Athena love and hate?" Jeno asked.

"We know she hates vampires," Hector said. "Sorry, but it's true, or she wouldn't have collapsed the caves beneath her temple."

"Fair enough," Jeno said.

"And she loves the arts, especially crafting and good music," Hector added. "She also loves to help damsels in distress."

"Unless they're being raped in her temple," Gertie said.

Hector stopped pacing. "We need another god on our side. Maybe I should ask my father to help."

Gertie jumped up. "I have an idea! Maybe we could convince Hephaestus to create a shield identical to Athena's."

"And then we make a switch!" Hector said.

Gertie smiled and crossed her arms. "Exactly."

Then she became aware of the chemistry between them and frowned. She didn't want to hurt Jeno. Had she blocked that thought, or had she left it unguarded?

Jeno was frowning, too, but said. "Good idea."

Before they could discuss their plan further, they were startled by the sudden appearance of Charon. He stood at the stern of his boat with a long pole in his bony old hands.

"Come on and board, already," he said in the raspy voice of an old man. "I don't have all day."

They stepped in and sat down, and then the grumpy old god pushed off from the bank and moved on.

"It's amazing to meet you," Gertie said after sitting in silence for a few moments, adjusting to the enormity of what was actually happening. She'd read so many stories about the ferryman, but the stories were never really about him at all. He was a mysterious character who transported the dead from the world of the living to the Underworld, and that was the extent of his tale. "Exceptional, really," she gawked, unable to take her eyes off the figure at the back of the boat with his long slender pole and long peasant robes.

"Not so exceptional," he said. "Every mortal eventually does."

"But I'm not a mortal…anymore," she said, and the wave of melancholy washed over her again.

Charon steadied the boat as they turned with the flowing river where it intersected another. "So, you're a vampire, then?"

Gertie nodded.

"*They* are," Hector clarified. "I'm not. I'm a son of Hephaestus."

Charon ignored Hector. "When you vampires came into being, I thought, 'Now here's my chance.' But it wasn't to be."

"What chance?" Jeno asked.

"Please tell us your story," Gertie asked. "The books are always so silent on the details of your life."

"That's because I never wanted a story of my own," he said. "And besides, we're almost to the gate."

Charon turned the boat onto another river that led to the gigantic black iron gate, and standing just outside was the three-headed dog Gertie knew to be Cerberus. Up through the chasm about a hundred yards beyond the gate, bright light shone down onto the river.

"It's daytime," Jeno said.

"We'll be scorched," Gertie added. "Oh, please don't make us go out there yet, Charon. I can't take another agonizing flight in the sun."

"I hate the rays of Helios, too," Charon said. "I suppose if you stay quiet, you can remain on the boat until nightfall, when my sister, Hemera, sleeps, and my mother and father embrace."

"Thank you," Jeno said.

"Your mother and father?" Gertie asked. "Your mother is Nyx, the goddess of night, right?"

Charon nodded.

"And your father?"

"Erebus, the foggy, ethereal mists of oblivion."

"And Hemera?" Gertie asked. "I don't think I've read about her. What is she?"

"Day," Charon said. "Each morning, she parts my parents' embrace."

"How did you get to be the ferryman of the Underworld?" Gertie asked.

"I told you to sit quietly," Charon said. "No one has ever asked me such questions. And it's not in my nature to answer them."

"But I have so many," Gertie said. "Like why do you look so old when every other god looks young? And are you married? Have any children? And why are you the ferryman? Did Hades choose you?"

"All your chatter reminds me why I chose to work with the dead," Charon said.

Ouch. Gertie clamped her mouth shut.

Then to her great surprise, Charon continued, "After my mother gave birth to me, I wandered with my father for many years as part of his ethereal mist, entering into the recesses of every dark corner to spy on the creation of the world. As the earth formed and it was populated with people, my parents asked me what job I would like—everyone had to have a job.

"I didn't know. There were too many choices back then, as we were among the first beings in existence. And I was told that once I chose, I couldn't change my mind. I had ten years to decide. I wandered the earth, lonely as a cloud.

"One thing I noticed—I enjoyed both mortals and immortals. I didn't talk much, but I enjoyed watching others. I was fascinated by their stories. I realized early on that I would rather hear the stories of other people's lives than live out my own adventures. I was a voyeur, like my parents. I ate up other people's histories."

This had been true of Gertie, too, up until recently. Even now she wondered if she would rather be *living* or *reading* the life she was leading now.

"Since I found daylight uncomfortable, the Underworld seemed like a logical place for me. As the ferryman for the dead, I would have privy to every human ever made, and I could absorb their stories as my own, since they were moving onto the River of Forgetfulness, anyway, and would no longer remember them.

"But as the years wore on, and the tragedies of their lives were revealed to me again and again, I realized the true burden I had undertaken. You want to know why I appear old? It's because I have been worn down by the stories of every mortal to board this vessel. If I could ever break away, I might look and feel young again."

Gertie felt her eyes stretch wide. She was surprised, first, that the god had said so much, and second, that he shared his dream of breaking away. "Could that ever happen?"

"Aye, if I could find another to take my place," he said.

But who would do that?

"When the vampires first came into being," he continued, "I thought I saw my chance. I thought the living dead would populate the realm of Hades and share in the burden of caring for the dead. I imagined vampires meeting the dying, draining their bodies of blood, and then bringing their souls to their judgment and final destination. I could become more of an overseer, with the time to have a life of my own, to unburden myself of the stories of others and begin my own tale. But, as you know, that didn't come to be."

At that moment, they neared the iron gates, which opened. All three heads of the dog growled at them as they passed. Gertie trembled at the prospect of meeting the sunlight up ahead, but before they reached it, a flurry of another kind of light descended onto the boat. Gertie blinked and in a moment was able to recognize the god she had seen during her first visit to the Underworld. It was Thanatos, the god of death, and with him were three transparent souls.

"Charon?" the boy god asked—he looked no older than Hector.

"Vampires," the ferryman said as he swung his skiff back toward the gate.

Gertie felt funny, like she was losing all her strength.

"*They* are." Hector pointed to Gertie and Jeno. "I'm a son of Hephaestus."

As soon as he had spoken, Hector fainted.

"Hector?" Gertie found it hard to breathe.

"You can't be here," the boy god said. "You need to go back to the Upperworld."

"But the sunlight hurts us," Gertie said.

"That's better than what will happen if you remain in this boat," the god of death said.

"Let's go," Jeno said. "Before we get too weak to fly."

Jeno and Gertie each grabbed one of Hector's arms, and together they hurled themselves into the daylight and into the nearest shelter they could find. It was a barn full of pigs and cows, and they had landed in a loft in a bed of hay.

They startled a small boy who was milking a cow below. Without seeing what had made the noise, he jumped from his stool and scurried away.

CHAPTER SIXTEEN

The Barn

Can we just rest here for a little bit?" Gertie asked, flat on her back on the pad of hay. "I'm tired and hungry and need to think."

Hector, who had landed between the two vampires and was only just coming to after passing out, slowly sat up, like a drunken sailor, and asked, "What just happened?"

"Thanatos," Jeno explained. "Anyone who's not a god basically dies in his presence."

"But *we're* immortal, right?" Gertie asked of Jeno. "So why did I feel like I was dying, too?"

Jeno rolled over onto his side and propped his head up with his elbow. "The gods can be swallowed and digested and still emerge years later fully grown, but *we* can be destroyed. *We* can die."

Gertie knew that all too well, especially after what had happened to Homer and the ninety-seven other vampires who had died recently. Especially after what had happened to Calandra.

"Right," she said.

Hector lay back down on his back. "I vote for resting. I almost died back there. Wow."

"I'm going to die if I don't get a drink soon," Gertie complained.

"Go for it," Hector said, without opening his eyes. "Jeno, too. Just save a little for me, man."

Gertie sat up and met Jeno's eyes over Hector's body lying between them.

"We could each take a single draw, to hold us over until tonight," Jeno said.

"You go first," Gertie said. "It's been ages since you've fed."

Hector began to snore.

"Let's let him sleep first," Jeno said. "He's exhausted."

As starving as she was, Gertie nodded. "Okay. You're right."

"Maybe we should all try to rest." Jeno rolled onto his back and closed his eyes.

Gertie lay back down, too, but she couldn't sleep because she was too hungry. She wondered if she could drink the blood of one of the animals in the barn.

"You *can*," Jeno said, "but it's disgusting."

"It can't be that bad." She thought of Louis in *The Vampire Chronicles* and Edward in *Twilight*.

"Oh, trust me. It's like the worst vegetable you've ever eaten combined with the stalest bread, the moldiest cheese, the most putrid fruit…"

"Okay, I get it."

They lay there in silence for a while, listening to Hector's snoring, until they both sensed a presence outside. Gertie sat up as the barn door creaked open and a slant of light shone down below. The little boy had returned. He went back to his stool and to the milking of the cow, but Gertie could read his thoughts, and he was listening for what he had heard earlier in the loft. He seemed to suspect a flock of birds had come to roost—at least that's what his mother had told him had probably happened.

Gertie was surprised the mother hadn't come to see for herself, but she supposed most mortals would take a story of something flying into the barn loft as either a child's imagination or a flock of birds.

She wondered what the boy thought of Hector's gentle snoring. Maybe he couldn't hear it down there.

"Sorry, Zelda," the boy said to the cow in Greek. "Is that better?"

The cow, of course, did not reply.

"Mamá doesn't believe in ghosts, but you and I know the truth," the boy said. "And if there are any ghosts in this barn, they should know not to mess with me, right, Zelda? And if there are any robbers or murderers or criminals, they shouldn't mess with me, either. I'm like a ninja. I know karate and judo, and I am *strong*."

Gertie covered her mouth to stifle her giggles. She glanced over at Jeno to see him smiling with his eyes closed.

After several more minutes of the boy's chatter to his cow, the scent of blood spilled up toward the rafters and hung, palpable, in the loft with Gertie. He must have cut himself. A check to his mind confirmed he had cut his finger on the rusty lip of the bucket. The boy licked at his finger, but the aroma filled the barn, and Gertie's mouth watered.

She turned to Jeno and told him telepathically, *I'm going to talk him into letting me feed from him. I'm starving. Please don't try to stop me.*

Five more hours until dusk. Can't you wait? Go to sleep.

I'm too hungry to sleep. I'm going down.

Let's wake Hector instead, Jeno said. *Leave the boy alone.*

I can't. We might need Hector's blood later tonight—I might need it. I want him strong for our quest.

Leave the poor boy alone, Jeno said again. *He's already frightened.*

I'll be nice.

As soon as Gertie climbed to her feet, the board beneath her creaked, and the boy below froze.

Jeno sat up and threw Gertie one more look of disapproval before she lifted off her feet and hovered in the air. Then, like a flash, she flew to the barn door, putting a few cows between her and the boy, who sat stiff and still on his stool and was no longer milking the cow.

"I'm not going to hurt you," Gertie said gently.

The boy didn't move. After a beat, he said. "I knew I wasn't imagining things."

He was probably nine or ten years old—about Phoebe's age. "You have nothing to fear."

"That's what all the bad guys say just before they kill you." The boy kept his eyes on his cow.

Gertie laughed. "What are you talking about?"

"I watch TV. I know how this is going down. Why else would you be here? I don't have any money, so you don't want to rob me."

"No. I don't want to rob you."

"You must be one of those serial killers who hunt down kids."

"I'm not a serial killer."

"Then a one-time killer. You just want to kill *me*."

"I don't want to kill you."

"I'd rather be killed than raped."

That caught Gertie off guard. Images of Alexander burned through her skull. "Oh, my God. I'm not going to do anything like that."

"Then what?"

What the heck am *I doing?* "Nothing. I was just tired and needed a safe place to rest."

He finally looked at her. "What are you?"

"A teenager. I'm just a regular teenaged girl." She locked onto his eyes and moved forward, mesmerizing him.

"But I saw something fly in. I heard you fall."

"No, you didn't." She moved past the cows.

"Maybe I didn't."

"I'm just a regular kid, like you." She stepped directly in front of him.

"Like me."

"So, thank you for letting me use your barn to get some rest." She put her hand on his shoulder.

"You're welcome."

"I want to thank you with a hug. Okay?"

He nodded.

Gertie's mouth watered as she leaned in, put her arms around the little boy, and then sank her fangs into his soft, sweaty throat. Tears sprang to her eyes. She was as bad as the women in the city, and she couldn't seem to stop herself.

The warm liquid burst into her mouth and quenched her thirst. She decided she might as well take a full pint, so she could afford to spare Hector later, but before she had swallowed down half that, she sensed a presence outside the barn door.

Gertie, get out of there! Jeno cried.

From the corner of her eye, she saw Jeno looking down at her with a frown.

Unable to stop herself from taking a few more quick draws at the boy's neck, Gertie was burned by the light when the barn door flung open, and a woman screamed.

Gertie panicked and also screamed, standing frozen like the boy in the shadow of a cow. While Gertie was paralyzed with shock, the stout woman grabbed a shovel and bashed the end of it against Gertie's head. Jeno dropped down like a streak of lightning and bit the woman on her bulky arm, to paralyze her.

Hector peered down from the loft just as Gertie and Jeno descended on the woman, both drawing from a different arm as the boy beat against them with his fists.

The boy, infused with the strength from the vampire virus, was hurting Gertie, along with one ray of sunlight burning her leg. Just as Hector shouted from above, Gertie turned and hissed at the boy with a mouth full of fangs and blood.

The boy shrank back from her in fear and revulsion.

She looked up to see Hector do the same.

Then Hector leapt from the loft, believing he could still fly, and landed on Gertie, who tried her best to break his fall. Jeno had stupefied the woman and had now locked eyes with the boy, making him forget all that had happened. Telepathically, he commanded the mother and son to leave the barn, close the door, and return to their farmhouse to sleep.

Once they were gone, Hector recovered from his fall and took several steps away from the two of them, looking at them with the same fear and revulsion the boy had shown on his face. "How could you?"

Gertie stepped toward him. "Hector…"

He backed away from her, holding his palms up. To Jeno, he said, "Just when I thought we were friends. Just when I thought I could trust you."

"Let me explain," Gertie said, wiping her mouth with the back of her hand.

"Man!" He pointed an accusatory finger at Jeno. "What have I gotten myself into? How did I end up on your side?"

"This wasn't Jeno's fault. He tried to stop me."

"That's not what I saw," Hector said.

"He only went after the woman because she attacked me. You've got to believe me. Jeno is innocent."

Jeno stepped forward and said, "Let me talk."

"I'm listening," Hector said.

"It's true. I tried to stop Gertie, but I shouldn't have."

"What?" Gertie shook her head. "I was wrong, not you. I was starving, and I gave into temptation."

"This is what we are," Jeno said. "I've been fighting it for centuries. We all have—those of us who want to obey the laws. But this is who we are and what we do. We can't keep denying that."

Hector raked a hand through his hair. "So I'm supposed to accept that? I'm supposed to just stand by while you attack humans?"

"No," Jeno said. "You're meant to protect humans."

"So now we're back to being enemies? I thought you were my friend."

"I *am* your friend," Jeno said. "You're a good man, and I'm honored that you would think of me that way. It means a lot to me."

Hector shook his head again. "But…"

"Just let me talk," Jeno insisted. "This is why we need change. Vampires need a new way of life. They need to be able to be true to themselves without threatening the human race."

"How?" Gertie asked. "You mean what Charon said?"

"Hades said it, too," Jeno pointed out. "We are the dead. We belong to the Underworld. We have been trying to survive up here where the sun hurts and destroys us, where people hate us, and where gods punish us for things that we can't help."

"Would your father agree?" Gertie asked. "Would he lead the other vampires to serve in the Underworld?"

"He's been talking about freedom," Jeno said. "I doubt I can convince him to choose servitude."

"So, what does this mean?" Hector asked. "What are you saying to me, Jeno?"

"I wish I knew, brother." Jeno crossed the room to sit on a bale of hay. "Vampires are like Medusa. We were the victims of the Maenads, and yet we're also the ones being punished."

"But if the vampires embrace their true nature," Hector said, "Well, we're all screwed."

"This isn't about good versus evil," Gertie said. "I know that."

"And it's not about right or wrong," Jeno said. "Neither side has the higher moral ground. The vampires didn't ask for this and shouldn't be punished, and the gods need to protect human life."

"So, what's it about?" Hector said. "If this uprising isn't about good versus evil or right versus wrong, what's it about?"

"Maybe together we can figure it out." Jeno stood and extended his hand. It hung there for a few moments before Hector leaned in and took it. Gertie sighed with relief.

"Okay," Hector said. "Let's figure this out together."

Gertie added her hand to the pair, and they all shook on it.

CHAPTER SEVENTEEN

The Vigil

Since Gertie and Jeno would be stuck in the barn until dusk, Hector made the journey alone to his father's temple to beg for help, stopping by his house first for food, new clothes, a candle, and his ukulele.

Gertie and Jeno lay side by side on the hay in the loft and closed their eyes. Jeno reached out and held her hand, so she took it, but she guarded her thoughts and kept a little distance because she was completely confused about her feelings for the two boys. It wasn't fair to either of them for her to be in love with both. She had to choose, and she couldn't. Since she was a vampire, the obvious choice was Jeno; but a strong desire to be with Hector wouldn't let her make it.

Now that she was full, Gertie was sleepy, so she invited Hypnos, the god of sleep, to take her.

When she awoke, it was nighttime, and Jeno was already awake, waiting for her. Since they were both full from the boy's mother, they flew straight to Hephaestus's temple to find Hector.

On the way, Jeno said, "My father thinks we are foolish."

"He knows our plan?"

"Only that we have to do a favor for Hades."

"How. Did he speak to you telepathically?"

"Yeah, while you were sleeping. I told him we were caught, and a deal was made, but not the details. I told him we weren't allowed to say."

"And he was okay with that?"

"He said we had one week to deliver the helm."

"Do you think we're being foolish?"

"No."

"Have you been able to talk to Phoebe or Damien?" Gertie asked. She had tried without success.

"Phoebe must have quickly learned to block her mind," Jeno said. "And Damien's mind seems to be tied to my father's."

"What do you mean?"

"It's like he doesn't have many independent thoughts. He uses my father's mind to interpret the world around him."

"Like he did with Phoebe's," Gertie said, piecing it together. He must be too young to have developed a complete mind of his own before he was turned. "I hope they're okay. I promised Mamá…"

"I know."

They reached the acropolis and descended near the temple of Hephaestus. Inside, they found Hector sitting on the stone floor in front of a lighted pillar candle strumming his ukulele. Beside him were three empty fast-food bags.

"No sign of him yet?" Jeno asked.

"Nothing," Hector said.

"What if he never answers?" Gertie sat beside him on the floor. "Vladimir's given us a week."

"My mom said that if you can keep a vigil at his temple for three days straight, he will come," Hector said.

"Have you tried this before?" Jeno asked, getting comfortable on the floor beside them, so that they made a ring around the candle.

"Dozens of times when I was younger," Hector answered. "But every time, I got hungry and gave up after the second day. And then, when I got older, well, I didn't want to seem desperate. I was too proud."

"Then how do we know it'll work?" Gertie asked.

"My mom's done it three times, and all three times, he came."

Gertie wasn't completely convinced, but since she had no better ideas, they sat together and waited. They killed time by telling stories, but they weren't happy ones.

Hector told about the first time he met his father. At the age of seven, Hector had been staying with a neighbor while his mother had been on a three-day vigil. Usually good at keeping her feelings for Hephaestus to herself, she'd returned sobbing, quivering, and broken. Hector became so angry, that he took off running, barefoot and in his pajamas, from their neighborhood for the acropolis. Only his mother was fast enough to catch him, but she was too weak, both physically and emotionally, to do so.

"It was the dead of night," Hector said. "Tramps—I'm sorry, vampires—were out. I could sense them. But I didn't care. I just ran and ran until I reached my father's temple. Then I climbed to the very top." Hector pointed up. "I stood on the highest point and threatened to destroy his temple."

"Oh my God," Gertie said. She could imagine it so vividly: Hector a little boy in his pajamas on the top of this temple, throwing a tantrum to get the attention of his father. "He showed up?"

"Only after I stomped so hard, I put a crack in this place," Hector said.

Jeno and Gertie laughed.

"Then what happened?" Jeno asked.

"He picked me up with his golden claw and sat me on his back, right between his wings. I was scared to death."

Gertie recalled the night the giant crane had carried her and Hector from the sea. "Did he say anything?"

"A sword and shield appeared in my hands, which scared me even more, because I couldn't hold on with anything but my legs. I'd never flown through the sky like that. It was amazing and terrifying."

Gertie remembered the first time she'd ever flown with Jeno. "I know what you mean."

Jeno must have read her thoughts. He looked at her and smiled.

"My father told me I had to be brave and help my mother," Hector went on. "He said *he* had to help *all* people. It was his duty as a god. But *my* responsibility was my mother. Then he flew me home."

"Did you ever find out what had made her so upset?" Gertie asked.

"Not until I was twelve. She sat me down one night and explained how my father had been tricked into being with her. She'd found out that night when I was seven. All those years, she'd assumed my father loved her but couldn't be with her because he was a god, and she was a mortal. But then, she missed him so much, she had just wanted to see him one more time."

"Your father was tricked?" Jeno asked.

Hector nodded. "Artemis was mad at Apollo and thought she'd get her revenge by tricking Hephaestus into sleeping with one of Apollo's daughters."

"The gods can be so petty," Jeno said.

"It's true," Hector agreed. "They can be really selfish."

"That's true of humans and vampires, too," Gertie said. "It's true of me." She thought of the boy and his mother in the barn.

Jeno wrapped his arms around his knees and leaned back. "Good point, but there is no group more selfish than the Maenads."

"They don't seem to know any better," Gertie said. "You don't blame her, do you?" Gertie meant Jeno's mom.

"No, but the first time I saw her, when she came to our house, drunk on the wine of Dionysus—I'll never get that night out of my head. Calandra and I were at the table eating dinner with our father. My mother had been gone for a few weeks, visiting her sister in a city then known as

Thebes. Before we'd finished our dinner, my mother came into the house. We were relieved to see her, but she looked different."

"Did she say anything?" Gertie asked.

Jeno shook his head. "She screeched in a strange voice and charged my father. Calandra and I tried to stop her, but she had superhuman strength. I couldn't believe my eyes. After she had finished tearing apart my father, she went to work on Calandra. I jumped on my mother's back and wrapped my hands around her throat, trying to strangle her. But she tore my poor sister apart and then turned on me."

Gertie shuddered. "How could Dionysus allow that to happen?"

Jeno shrugged. "The king of Thebes didn't recognize Dionysus as a god and didn't like the dancing near his city."

"So, Dionysus got revenge?" Gertie wanted her father to be better than that.

"Not at first," Jeno said. "He sent Tiresias and even went himself to explain, but King Pentheus was blinded by his own rage, they say. So Dionysus allowed the Maenads to drift into the city from the woods."

"That's terrible," Gertie said.

"All the women were converted, including my aunt and mother. The men and children were destroyed."

"I've never really heard the story," Hector said. "Not exactly."

"Many cities in Greece were affected when the Maenads wandered. Dionysus was too drunk himself to recognize what he had allowed to take place."

Tears fell from Gertie's eyes.

"Don't cry," Jeno said. "It was a long time ago."

"I think Dionysus is my father," she blurted out.

Hector's mouth fell open and he jumped to his feet, nearly putting out the candle. "What? Gertie, why would you think that?"

"We overheard her mother talking to Marta Angelis," Jeno explained.

Hector started pacing. "My mother must know. That explains why she was working so hard to negotiate with the vampires for your return. I thought it was because she knew how I felt about you, but this makes more sense. She wanted to save a fellow demigod."

Gertie sat back on her hands. "You never told me she was negotiating with the vampires."

"Well, once we learned you'd been turned…" Hector's voice trailed off.

"She just gave up?" Gertie asked.

"No," Jeno answered for him. "But they could no longer negotiate for you."

"Why not?" Gertie asked, trying to puzzle it all out.

"Because as soon as you turned, the mission changed," Hector explained.

"The mission became killing my father," Jeno said.

Gertie felt the blood leave her face. "Oh."

She noticed Hector had turned white, too.

"What makes you think it's Dionysus?" Jeno asked, changing the subject.

Gertie leaned forward with her legs crossed and her boots tucked close to her body. "Think about it. Dionysus is known for losing himself in his wine. I do the same with my books. He's addicted to wine like I'm addicted to reading. He's also an outsider and unloved by his parents, like me."

"Zeus loves him," Hector said.

"But he doesn't stand up for him very often, does he?" Gertie challenged.

"I guess not." Hector rejoined them on the floor in their circle around the candle. "So, you're a vampire *and* a demigod. Wow."

"And she's the daughter of the lord of the vampires," Jeno added. "Crazy."

Gertie shifted back to lean on her hands. "Well, I don't know for sure…"

"That's why he saved us," Jeno said. "That's why he stopped the vampires from killing you and Hector. Were you praying to him when that happened?"

Gertie nodded.

"That's a pretty solid sign," Hector said.

"But he's such a douche bag," Gertie said. "He just gets drunk all the time and doesn't seem to care about anything but himself. The vampires had to wait days and days for him to finally tell them what to do, and even then, it's all been so cryptic."

"He's a champion of the underdog and a patron of the arts," Hector said defensively.

"He's a douche bag," Gertie repeated. "Just like the father who raised me. And just like your father, Jeno."

"Don't say that," Jeno said.

She climbed to her feet, needing to stretch her legs. "When he couldn't handle being a vampire, he abandoned you and Calandra. And now that he's back, look how he's treating you."

"I betrayed him."

"Because he was wrong. And because you love me."

There was an awkward silence as Gertie blushed again.

"Even Hephaestus could be a better father," she said. "Let's face it."

"Don't say that here," Hector warned.

Tears sprang to her eyes again. "Babá—I mean Nico Angelis—has been the only real father I've ever known, and now he wants nothing to do with me."

Hector reached for her hand and squeezed it. "That's not true. He still loves you."

She squeezed his hand back but then pulled it away to wipe her eyes. She didn't want Jeno to feel uncomfortable.

"Have you figured out your hidden talents yet?" Jeno asked, changing the subject again.

"I don't have any," she said.

"Of course, you do," Hector said. "All demigods do."

Maybe she was the exception.

"Listen," Jeno climbed to his feet beside Gertie. "It's almost dawn. We need to go."

"Where?" Hector asked, climbing to his feet, too.

"The barn, I guess. It's not too far and no one will bother us there." Jeno offered his hand to Hector. "See you at dusk."

Hector took his hand and shook it. "See you then."

Gertie gave Hector a hug and said, "See you tonight."

As she and Jeno were about to fly away, Hector called out, "Can you guys bring me some food tomorrow? Maybe a burger and fries? Make that two burgers and fries? And a Dr. Pepper? I'm not sure if my mom will be able to make it."

He grabbed his wallet from his back pocket and pulled out some money.

Gertie laughed at Hector's craving for American fast-food and took the money. "I guess a guy's gotta eat."

CHAPTER EIGHTEEN

Gertie's Hidden Talent

Gertie and Jeno reached the barn just as the first rays of the sun broke through the clouds.

"Too bad we don't know Charon's sister personally," Gertie said as she took a seat on a bale of hay. "Maybe we could persuade her not to part her parents' embrace."

Jeno laughed as he sat beside her. Then he moved a strand of her hair behind her ears.

"What are you guarding from me?" she asked.

"Have you ever noticed that your book addiction helps you as much as it hurts you?" He gave her a tender smile.

She thought about that.

He lifted her chin with his index finger. "Maybe you do get lost in books to avoid reality. I do it, too. But if you weren't such an avid reader, you wouldn't have figured out who your father was, or what we needed to gain leverage in the uprising, or how to get it. The knowledge you've gained from books has been your most powerful weapon."

Gertie smiled back at him. "Thank you, Jeno."

"That duality is the same for Dionysus. The wine acts as both his weakness and his power."

"I wish he did more good than harm."

"He's helped a lot of groups over the years. Now he's trying to do the same for the vampires."

"Why do you suppose he's waited so long to help you?"

"Maybe he was waiting for you." He gently nudged her with his shoulder.

"I doubt that. I don't even have any hidden talents."

"I think you're wrong."

"Until I became a vampire, I was completely powerless," she argued. "I was nothing before I was turned. I should be grateful."

"But you aren't," he said sadly. She started to apologize but he said, "No. I understand. I feel the same way. I've never liked being a vampire."

"It does have its high points," she said. "I love to fly. I love being strong. And I love being able to see you naked."

She had wanted to lighten the mood, and it worked. Jeno busted out laughing.

"I think you have a hidden power." Jeno smoothed another strand of hair away from her face. "You're so beautiful, koureesti mou."

She blushed. "So are you, Jeno, but beauty isn't power."

"It can be. In fact, it's very important to the success of a vampire, but that's not the power I'm talking about."

"Then what?"

"There have been other children of Dionysus, and I knew one in particular."

"Who?"

"He was a potter. He made the most beautiful wine jugs the world had ever seen."

"Was that his only talent?"

"No. Normally, he was a humble potter turning clay into ceramic masterpieces. But when he drank wine, he became a powerful being."

Gertie furled her brow. "He'd get drunk and what, turn into the incredible hulk?"

"Not drunk. It only took one sip. Have you ever had wine before?"

"Not until that night of the dance, with the Maenads and satyrs. That was my very first drink."

"Did anything happen?"

"I just got dizzy and…well, I figured out who my father was."

"Tonight, we need to get you some wine."

She smiled. "I really do love you, you know."

"I know." He kissed her cheek. "But I'm not the only man who has your heart. I'll keep my distance until I am."

She frowned and felt a little nervous now. "I'm sorry."

"You can't help how you feel, but Hector won't be around forever, and you and I will."

She quickly blocked her mind, because the thought emerging would only hurt him: What if the demigods were successful in their mission to kill Vladimir?

"I know what you're thinking," he said. "I don't need to hear your thoughts to know."

"What if they kill him?"

"Too many vampires need him to stay alive. I don't see it happening."

"Good," she said, though her stomach clenched. Sometimes she hoped the demigods *were* successful. She missed being human, especially when she was hungry, like she was now.

If only a burger and fries sounded good like it used to.

That night, they flew to Omonoia Square to feed on their human contacts. Then they went into an American burger joint to get Hector's food. Before they left the downtown area, Jeno went to a liquor store, and using Hector's change, bought a bottle of wine.

"Are you sure about this?" Gertie asked, as they flew toward the acropolis.

"It might be the only way to find out your hidden talent."

When they arrived at the Temple of Hephaestus, they found Hector curled on his side, asleep, holding his ukulele in his arms like a lover.

They held off waking him, knowing he needed rest, but the smell of the food aroused him.

"I'm starving," he said as he opened his eyes. "Thanks. I missed you guys."

Jeno and Gertie exchanged smiles.

As Hector eagerly ate the burgers and fries, Gertie checked his mind and learned that the day had been hectic for him, with all the tourists visiting and asking Hector questions. When approached by strangers, he had explained he was holding a vigil for the god of the forge, hoping for an answer to his prayers. Some of the tourists had been respectful and had left him alone. Others had kept asking him more annoying questions. Still others thought he was playing his ukulele for tips and expected him to sing.

Most of the tourists hadn't been happy about the state of the acropolis. With all the loud construction going on and many of the ruins destroyed, the general mood had been irritable at best.

"Tough day?" Gertie asked.

Hector nodded as he gulped down his food. "Tough crowd, too."

"Well, they're gone now," Gertie said, reassuringly. "And we only have one more day to go."

"So, what's with the bottle of wine?" Hector asked after sipping down some of the Dr. Pepper.

Jeno extended the nail of his index finger and pierced the cork before popping it off. "This is how we're going to discover Gertie's hidden talent."

Gertie explained Jeno's theory to Hector.

"As long as we don't have too much of it," Hector warned. "We need to keep our heads on straight if we expect to have any chance of pulling off this mission."

"Believe me," Jeno said, handing the bottle to Gertie. "The mission is important to me. I won't do anything to jeopardize it. Just take a sip, Gertie."

The wine wasn't as smooth going down as the sip from the golden cup the night of the dance. It also wasn't as delicious. In fact, it tasted horrible. But as with that night, the dizziness built up, from her chest to her head, in a way that reminded her of the first time Jeno had bitten her.

She lay on her back on the hard, stone floor, and felt like a little girl again, spinning in the backyard behind her parents' New York mansion.

"Gertie?" Jeno asked.

Gertie could only smile and close her eyes.

"Do you feel anything?" Hector asked.

She must have fallen asleep, because she began to dream of an enormous golden snake looking down at her. The snake balanced a clay jar on the end of its tail and lowered the jar to her. She took it between her hands and drank. It was more wine. Delicious wine. Smooth, like her father's.

"Gertie, are you okay?" Jeno asked.

"You're freaking us out." Hector gently slapped at her cheeks.

"I'm okay," she said, blinking. "Did I fall asleep?"

"No. You were talking," Hector said. "You mentioned my father, but I couldn't make out the rest."

"I was dreaming of a golden snake," she said, still trying to get her bearings. Boy, oh boy, had the world revolved around her this time. "He gave me some of my father's wine."

"Maybe it means something," Jeno said. "Maybe it was a vision."

"Big ol' snake," she said. "Huge. But not scary."

"Can you remember anything else?" Hector asked.

Gertie blinked a few more times. A new image flashed behind her lids: she and Hector were entangled in one another's arms, lying on his bed, and passionately kissing. He was saying he loved her, and she was saying it back. She shook her head and tried to guard her mind from Jeno.

"I guess I'm tired," she said. "I should have slept some today."

"Go ahead," Hector said. "Jeno can keep me company."

Gertie closed her eyes, but she didn't sleep.

She could hear Jeno take a sip from the bottle. "Want some?"

"No, thanks," Hector replied. "But thanks a lot for bringing me food. Man, was I hungry."

"Did you get enough?" Jeno asked.

"Oh, yeah. Maybe too much." Hector laughed.

"Well, no need to thank me. I'm the one who should be thanking you."

Hector cleared his throat. "Listen. I'm not doing this for you or for the vampires. I mean, I feel for you, man, but I have my own reasons."

"I know, but you could have taken Gertie and ran."

"Not with Phoebe and Damien still with your people."

The boys were quiet for a moment, but then Jeno asked, "So if Gertie and the Angelis kids weren't involved, and knowing what you know, would you side against the vampires in this uprising?"

Hector sighed. Gertie held her breath, not wanting to miss a word.

"Knowing what I know now," Hector said. "I might not go so far as to try to steal the helm or Athena's shield, but I'd speak up. I don't think I'd just sit by and do nothing."

"Most people do sit by and do nothing in the face of injustice, when it doesn't affect them," Jeno said. "But I can see you are different."

"How did you know about my dog? About Paris?" Hector asked suddenly.

"That wasn't long after I turned Damien. I'd been keeping an eye on Marta and her family. I had nothing better to do one evening, so I followed her kids to the park, where they met you and your dog the night he was hit."

"He was a good dog."

"I bet he was."

"I had him seven years and was nine when I got him."

"I've had a lot of pets throughout the centuries," Jeno said. "It never gets easier to say goodbye. Eventually, I stopped getting close."

"You don't like being a vampire much, do you?" Hector said more than asked.

"It's my affliction," Jeno said. "But I try to make the most of it."

"Have you ever thought about…?" Hector's voice dropped off, but his mind was an open book: *Suicide?*

"Of course."

"Seriously?"

"Yes. Many times. Two things have always prevented me from following through with it."

"What two things?"

"First of all, it goes against my instinct. I'm wired to survive at all costs."

"And what's the second thing? Love?"

Gertie felt Hector's eyes on her as he wondered if Jeno's love for her was keeping him alive.

"No, not love. Duty," Jeno said.

"Duty? To who?"

"The correct English is 'to whom.'"

"Seriously?"

"I know the language well."

"I mean are you seriously going to sit there and correct my grammar? Come on, man. That's not cool."

"Sorry. I was only trying to help."

Hector snorted. "So duty to *whom?*"

"To all the vampires I turned whose lives would be destroyed along with me. It's one thing to make the decision for myself, but…."

"Yeah. I see."

"And if you kill my father to save Gertie, at least thirty people will go with him."

"Including you?" Hector asked.

"No. Not me."

"Good."

"But wouldn't it be better for you if I went, too?" Jeno asked. Gertie felt his eyes move over her as Hector's had a moment ago.

"No, man," Hector said. "I'd be sad. We're friends now, right?"

"I hope so. But would a friend kill a friend's father?"

Hector was quiet for a few seconds. "Don't you want Gertie to be saved from what you call an affliction?"

"Not at the expense of my father's life. He's the only family I have left."

"You've forgiven him for wanting to kill Gertie? For making us go on this impossible mission?"

"I betrayed him."

"Because he was wrong."

"I'm not so sure of that."

"But human lives…"

"Maybe it's the only way to be heard," Jeno said. "I'm not so sure that getting Athena's shield to Hades is really going to solve anything for the vampires, to tell you the truth, but I'm willing to give it a try."

Hector seemed to be digesting that, as he was quiet again, until he said, "I don't think I'm going to need to kill your father."

Jeno said nothing as he read the rest of Hector's thought: *Because the council of demigods will do it for me.*

"So, I guess you don't want to be friends. I get that," Hector said.

"No, I do. I don't have very many. And I think if I were in your position, I'd feel the same way."

No one said anything for a few moments. Gertie was about to sit up, but then Hector spoke again.

"You really are a cool dude," Hector said. "I can see why she loves you."

Jeno didn't reply. Gertie tried really hard to read his mind, but it was heavily guarded.

Just then, they heard the swish of gigantic wings through the air as a white crane descended from the sky, like a second moon, luminous and beautiful.

They all three staggered to their feet, amazed that Hephaestus had actually come, and a day early at that. He swooped down and perched on the outside of his temple, waiting quietly.

"Father!" Hector cried.

"I sensed discord and urgency all around my temple," Hephaestus said. "What's this about?"

Hector told him about the vampires wanting the helm, their deal with Hades, and their idea to switch Athena's shield.

"Can you make one identical to hers?" Hector asked.

"Of course, I can," Hephaestus's voice bellowed from the golden beak. "But there is only one way such a quest can end, and that's with your deaths."

Gertie flinched. How could he be so sure?

Hephaestus continued: "The goddess of wisdom is the smartest among us and cannot be easily fooled. If she doesn't catch you making the switch, she will eventually recognize the trick. Then she'll hunt you down until you've all three been destroyed."

"What choice do we have?" Hector asked. "If we don't get the helm from Hades, Vladimir will kill Gertie and me. We die either way."

"You can rally the gods against the vampires," the giant crane said. "I mentioned this to you in our last meeting. Why have you joined forces with them?"

"Because they deserve freedom, like anyone else," Hector said. "Victims shouldn't be punished for the crimes committed against them."

Gertie glanced at Jeno, who smiled. His thoughts were still guarded, but she didn't need to read his mind to know what he was thinking. He was pleased that Hector had officially taken Jeno's side.

"You *can't* do this quest, my son," Hephaestus said. "Unless all three of you are willing to sacrifice your lives. Are you willing to do that?"

As Hector had said, what choice did they have? And maybe Hephaestus was wrong. Maybe they could pull it off and live.

They all three nodded.

Frightened, Gertie took each of the boys' hands, showing Hephaestus that they were united in their mission. "Can you think of any other way?"

"There is one person who could deceive Athena without incurring her wrath," Hephaestus said.

"Who?" Hector asked.

"My son, Erichthonius, also known as Erichtheus. His mother and I call him Erich."

"Who's that?" Gertie whispered to Hector. That was one god she hadn't read about.

Hector whispered, "Athena adopted him and has always loved him like a son."

"Athena adores him," Hephaestus said. "He can do no wrong in her eyes. If you can convince him to switch the shields, she'll forgive him when she learns the truth."

"How do we find him?" Jeno asked.

"Go to his temple around the corner, the Erichtheion," The giant crane replied.

"That temple was destroyed by Athena," Gertie said.

"Pray near the rubble. Entice him with your singing, Hector. He can't resist a beautiful voice." The great bird lifted from its perch and hovered in the air above them. "He appears as a golden snake."

Hector and Jeno gasped. Gertie felt the hair on the back of her neck prickle. Had her "dream" been a prophetic vision?

"Why would he help us?" Jeno asked. "Your son, Erechthonius. He has nothing to gain from it."

"Maybe there's something he wants." The bird hovered above, its luminosity blocking out the moon behind it. "I'll make the shield. You persuade Erich. I'll deliver the shield here tomorrow night."

The beautiful crane ascended into the sky and disappeared.

CHAPTER NINETEEN

The Golden Snake and the Golden Ram

As soon as the great crane was out of sight, Jeno turned to Gertie. "You can see the future! That's your talent!"

"This is brilliant!" Hector was full of excitement. "Maybe if she drinks more of that wine, she can tell us something about our mission, or the uprising, or anything we want to know."

"What did I say last time, exactly?" she asked, feeling uneasy. "You said I was mumbling."

"I couldn't make it out," Hector said. "Except for my father's name."

Blocking her mind, Gertie hoped she hadn't said anything about the passionate embrace with Hector.

"Did you see something else?" Jeno asked suspiciously. "Something you're not telling us?"

She shrugged. "Nothing important." Then she asked, "Do you really think I can see the future?"

Jeno squeezed her hand. "It seems so. Are you worried about something else you saw?"

She shook her head but, knowing she wasn't convincing, shuddered at the thought of hurting Jeno. How could she be with Hector anyway? She was a vampire.

Needing to change the subject, she turned to Hector. "So, what song are you going to sing to your brother the snake?"

"Oh, wow." Hector took a step back. "I guess he *is* my brother. That's new."

"No other demigods are from Hephaestus?" Gertie asked.

"Nope. I've been an only child my whole life. It'll be pretty cool to meet a sibling, even if he *is* a snake."

Gertie missed Nikita and sensed Jeno thinking about Calandra. "You okay?"

Hector bent his brows. "I'm so stupid. Sorry, man. I wasn't thinking. You just lost your sister."

"It's okay." Jeno picked up the bottle of wine and sat down on the floor, blowing out Hector's candle. Then he took a sip from the bottle. "So, are we ready to call the snake, then?"

"Hector needs to decide on a song before we head over there," Gertie said.

"I'll just sing my newest one," Hector said. "I wrote it when I thought I'd lost you forever, Gertie. That night you left with the vampires." His face turned red. "The words are fresh in my mind. I wrote it in English."

Gertie and Jeno each took an arm of Hector's and lifted him into the air toward the Erichtheion. Gertie's heart pounded against her rib cage the whole way. So many things could go wrong. So many things had already gone wrong.

When they reached the mound of rubble, Hector glanced at each of them and said, "Okay then. Here goes nothing." He took a deep breath and sang along to his ukulele (to hear Hector's song, go here: https://soundcloud.com/travispohler/alive-again):

I wish that I could feel alive again.
I don't know where, where I've been.
I've been away, away somewhere.

I surely wanted to stay,
But I went, and I died, I died that day.
One day … I tried to stay.

I would have died either way,
And now my life has gone astray,
And I have felt Death's embrace,
And I would like Death to delay,
And I would like to live another day.
One day … I want to stay.

I wish that I could feel alive again.
I don't know where, where I've been.
I've been away, away somewhere.

Tears formed in Gertie's eyes as she listened to Hector's soothing voice and heard the story of the pain she'd put him through when she'd flown away with Jeno that night they'd awakened Vladimir. All of Hector's pain and worry and sadness came through in his voice and in the words of his song. He'd been numb, not really alive.

Gertie could have listened to Hector's singing all night, but after twenty minutes he stopped and said, "I don't think he's coming."

"I saw it happen," Gertie said, desperate to see her vision come true. If it didn't, then maybe she had no talent, just as she had suspected all along.

"We need to be patient," Jeno said. "These things take time. Keep singing, Hector, It sounds nice."

"Maybe you should join me. Maybe all three of us should try it."

Gertie wasn't thrilled about Hector's idea. Her voice was more likely to frighten the god away.

"It's an interesting song for a vampire to sing," Jeno remarked. "It gives the lyrics a whole new meaning, but I'll give it a try."

Hector started up again, and Jeno joined. The two voices together sounded so lovely, and she didn't want to mess that up. She stood there, trying not to gawk at the most beautiful sight she'd ever seen: two gorgeous boys with equally gorgeous voices harmonizing beneath the stars on the acropolis. They each glanced at the other, grinning. They knew how good they sounded, and, worse, they could sense the affect they were having on Gertie. But Gertie wasn't embarrassed because her heart was warmed and overjoyed by their friendship. That was more important to her than anything.

Just when she had stopped thinking about the golden snake, it appeared, and Hector and Jeno quit their song.

"Who sssserenadesss me where my temple oncccce sssstood?" the golden snake hissed, reminding her of Kaa from *The Jungle Book*.

Hector stepped forward. "I'm a son of Hephaestus. My name is Hector, and these are my friends, Gertie and Jeno."

"A ssson of Hephaestusss?" the golden snake asked. "I've never heard of you."

Gertie read Hector's disappointment and wished there was something she could say, but he spoke again, "He was tricked into a union with my mother and doesn't like to speak of it."

"At leassst he had a *union* with your mother," the snake pointed out. "Gaia became my mother by default when my father sssspilled on her. She never cared much for me, you sssssee."

"I'm sorry to hear that," Hector said. "But I understand Athena loves you as her own."

"Yesss, but look what she hasss done to my temple," the snake hissed. "She said we had an infessstation that needed cleansssing, but I want my temple back!"

Gertie blanched at the word *infestation* and sensed Jeno's discomfort, too. Even Hector had turned a palcr shade of white. How could Athena be so insensitive? This further proved to Gertie that even the wisest of gods did not understand the vampires and their plight.

"Maybe we can help," Hector said.

Gertie cocked a brow. How could they help Erich?

"I'm lissstening," Erich hissed.

Hector crossed his arms. "How would you like to get Athena back by playing a little trick on her?"

"Hmmm. I'm ssstill lissstening."

"Hephaestus is making a shield identical to hers. He'll deliver it to his temple tomorrow night. We want you to switch them and bring us the real one."

"Intersssting. And what will you do with the real one, ssson of Hephaestusss?"

"We'll eventually give it back," Jeno said. "But before we do, we will give it to Hades, for safekeeping."

"Yesss. Good idea. She never goesss to the Underworld."

"So, we have a deal?" Hector asked.

"Oh, yesss!"

The three teens made it back to Hector's house just before dawn was about to break. Hector was disappointed to find his mother wasn't at home. A text from her revealed that she and the council of demigods were on a mission, and she couldn't disclose her location. Hector went around the house closing as many blinds and curtains as he could and told Gertie and Jeno to make themselves at home.

Gertie took a long hot shower upstairs in the guest bath, brushed her teeth, and put on a fresh pair of her own clothes, which almost made her feel human again.

Almost. Having to dodge the sunlight that broke through some areas of the house was a pretty clear reminder. The big window in the guest room had no blinds or curtains, so she had to avoid it.

Hector's bedroom, however, was protected by blinds. When she met up with the other two boys, they had also showered and were sitting side by side on the sofa in Hector's bedroom bent over Hector's smart phone, laughing.

They were watching a YouTube video and laughing so hard that tears welled in their eyes.

"That's got to be staged," Jeno said between laughs. "She can't be that stupid."

"It's not staged," Hector insisted. "She really is that dumb."

Gertie plopped in a cushy chair across from them. "You two sound like a couple of misogynists."

"This American YouTuber is having a debate over whether dogs have brains," Hector explained.

"I can't believe anyone her age can be that stupid," Jeno said again. "It's one thing when people argue whether or not dogs have souls. But brains? This has got to be a satire."

"I'm telling you, this girl is serious. That's what makes it so funny."

"Can I see?" Gertie asked.

Hector handed her the phone, and she replayed the video of a very blond girl with a fake tan, dark eye makeup, and enormous boobs on display in a very small bra. "You've got to be kidding me. This girl will do anything for attention, guys. Of course, she's not that stupid."

"Don't get mad," Hector said. "Why are you upset?"

"I'm not." But she was, even though she wasn't sure why. She handed the phone back to Hector and sighed.

Hector groaned. "Help me out here, Jeno. Are girls not a mystery?"

Jeno smiled. "I guess it's easier to understand them when you can read their minds."

"So, why's she mad?"

"She's not sure herself," Jeno said.

Hector stuffed his phone in his pocket. "Well, that doesn't help."

"I think she both pities and abhors the girl," Jeno said. "And somehow, this girl's behavior is the fault of all boys."

"How's it *our* fault?" Hector asked.

"Shut up, Jeno," Gertie said. "You're way off."

"You see this girl as both a victim and a threat," Jeno said. "Like a vampire."

"Give it a rest, Professor," Gertie said.

Hector turned to Jeno and started to whisper, but Jeno cut him off and said, "No, they don't."

"Did Hector just ask if girl vampires get their periods?" Gertie asked, on the edge of outrage.

"Not technically," Jeno said. "I stopped him before he actually said it."

"But he wondered it."

"Get out of my head," Hector said. "You can't get mad at me for wondering things."

"Oh, yes I can."

"Gertie," Jeno said softly. "Is something else bothering you?"

"No." She got up and crawled into Hector's bed, wishing she could fall asleep like a normal person.

"Maybe we should all get some rest," Hector said. "I'm beat."

"Good idea," Jeno said.

It *was* a good idea, especially for Hector, who needed more sleep. They'd be up again all night, as long as Erich didn't let them down.

"You take the couch, man," Hector said to Jeno. Then he snagged one of the pillows Gertie wasn't using and dropped it on the floor.

Gertie was about to tell Hector he could have his bed, but his thoughts revealed that he enjoyed the feel of the shag rug. As long as he was comfortable, she'd stay put.

She bit her lip and sighed and, not for the first time, wished she were back at the Angelis apartment living a normal life. She closed her eyes again and prayed to Hypnos, the god of sleep, and Morpheus, the god of dreams. Before she had finished, she also found herself praying to Dionysus—not so much praying as asking, "Do you care about me? Do I matter to you at all?"

It was still light outside when she woke up with Hector spooning her from behind.

What the heck?

She looked around the room to find Jeno sitting up on the sofa with his back to her.

He got up to use the bathroom about an hour ago, and when he returned, he crawled into his bed with you.

Jeno, I'm sorry.

I don't think he was awake enough to know what he was doing. He hadn't gotten much sleep during his vigil.

Gertie slowly lifted Hector's arm and crawled out of his embrace. Then she sat on the sofa with Jeno.

Did you get any sleep? she asked him.

A few hours. How about you? Do you feel rested?

Yes. But I'm so worried. Have you heard any news from your father? I still can't get through to Phoebe or Damien.

All I get are warnings from my father that we are running out of time.

Oh, Jeno. When will this ever end?

He patted her thigh. *Once we get the helm, once we get the help of Hades, maybe then.*

I hope so.

Do you want to take another sip of wine and see if you see anything?

Gertie was afraid, but she nodded.

Are you afraid of what you might see? he asked.

She shook her head and whispered, "I'm more afraid of not having a talent. The snake thing might have been a fluke. I don't want to let you and everyone else down."

Jeno kissed the tip of her nose. "Never."

She smiled back at him, wishing she felt as sure as he did.

Then Jeno grabbed the bottle of wine from Hector's desk and passed it over to her. She took a sip and sank back in the sofa, passing the bottle back. The room began to spin as the dizziness swept over her.

She was running through a thick forest toward something. The branches snapped into her face as she picked through them in the darkness. Then she heard voices up ahead. She dodged another tree, turned around a bend, and saw a bonfire up ahead, on the side of the mountain. She ran to it.

As she neared the fire, she recognized the faces of vampires encircling it. Maenads and satyrs were also present. Her father must be among them too. She searched and searched and cried out for him.

Then she heard a scream. Gertie plunged through the crowd to the center near the fire to find Hector's mother tied to a wooden post. Her wrists and ankles were bound with rope. Vladimir stood in front of her with a sword in his hand and Damien on his back. Before Gertie could say or do anything, Vladimir whipped the blade through the air and across Dori's neck, slicing off her head. Gertie flinched and screamed as the vampires crowded Dori's body to feed. They moved through Gertie like she wasn't even there, like her body was nothing but air.

Gertie tried to wake from the vision, but she couldn't. Not wanting to face the horrible sight before her, she turned to run away. On the outskirts of the crowd, waiting for her, was the golden ram, Dionysus.

Unlike the others in the vision, he looked at her like he saw her. Then he transformed from a ram into a man. He was large and muscular and beautiful, wearing a leather girdle and boots and a golden sword strapped across his chest.

"Why did you let them do that?" she asked him, as she caught her breath. "She was already tied up. She was no longer a threat. Why did they have to kill her?"

"This is war," the god said simply. "But now that you have seen it, maybe you can prevent it."

"You mean I have the power to alter my visions? They aren't set in stone?"

"Only the Fates can see what is certain," he said.

"Tell me what to do."

"Don't trust Hades."

Gertie was taken aback. "But we need the helm. We made a deal."

"When Erichthonius delivers Athena's shield to you, bring it to me at Mount Kithairon."

Gertie woke from the vision, gasping.

"Are you okay?" Jeno whispered.

She glanced at Hector's sleeping figure on the bed before meeting Jeno's gaze, feeling more confused than ever.

CHAPTER TWENTY

Athena's Shield

When Hector finally awoke a few hours later, Gertie described her vision to him.

"My mom!" He grabbed his phone from his desk and texted her. "Why didn't you wake me up right away?"

"It's not set in stone," Gertie said. "And we can't really do anything until nightfall." Gertie hadn't thought about texting Dori. Her stomach clenched as she glanced at Jeno. They should have woken up Hector hours ago.

"She's not replying. We have to get to Mount Kithairon. We have to go now!"

"So you think we should betray Hades?" Jeno asked.

"We don't have a choice," Hector said. "That vision sounds like a threat. It sounds like Dionysus is saying to bring him the shield, or else my mom gets killed."

Gertie crossed the room and put her hands on Hector's shoulders. "That's not how it felt. Now, calm down. We're not going to let anything happen to her. Okay?"

Hector took a deep breath. "Okay."

"But just to be safe, maybe you should go to Mount Kithairon and wait for me and Gertie to bring the shield," Jeno said. "Gertie should bite you, so you can fly there right away. She's probably starving, and we don't have time to stop and feed."

"I think we need to stick together," Gertie said. "What if Hector gets captured?"

"No, I think Jeno is right. Bite me, so I can keep in touch with you."

If Gertie had been told, "Bite me, so I can keep in touch with you," say, four months ago, she would have found the sentence to be nonsensical. But tonight, it made perfect sense.

"Are you sure, Hector?" she asked. "What if we need you to call Erich? What if we need you to sing?"

"She's got a point," Jeno said. "I didn't think about that. We'll be quick. All right, mate?"

He sighed. "Well, bite me anyway, so I can take off if I need to."

Gertie's mouth watered. She was hungry. For Jeno's sake, she probably should have drunk from Hector's wrist, but she wanted to comfort Hector. So she put her arms around his waist, kissed him on the cheek, and then quickly pierced his throat with her fangs.

She stopped herself at exactly eight ounces—a half pint.

Once Hector had recovered from the temporary paralysis, he grabbed his sword and his ukulele and said, "Let's go."

When they reached what was left of the Erichtheion, they were surprised by the sudden appearance of the golden snake. And balanced on the end of his tail was the shield of Athena.

"Brilliant!" Hector cried, reaching out for the shield.

"Not ssso fassst," Erich hissed. "Before I entrust you with this ssshield, I need to know you're worthy."

"But…" Gertie started to object and then held her tongue.

"Anssswer thisss riddle correctly, and the ssshield is yoursss, but only temporarily, of courssse."

The three teens glanced warily at one another.

"What walksss on four legsss in the morning, two in the afternoon, and three in the evening?" the snake asked.

"I know this one," Gertie whispered to the boys. "I've read this one a thousand times." Aloud to the snake, she said, "The correct answer is *man*. The morning is really a symbol for infancy, when a man crawls on all fours. The afternoon represents adulthood, when a man walks on two legs. And evening is old age, when he walks with a cane, or a third leg."

"Ssso it isss." Erich moved his tail forward and passed the golden shield to Gertie, just as he had passed her the jug of wine in her vision.

"Thank you!" she said, finding the shield to be much heavier than it looked.

The snake vanished as quickly as it had appeared.

"Let's go!" Hector said.

They flew northeast, toward Attica, and within minutes, the mountain came into view.

"There." Jeno pointed.

Gertie followed his finger to find the smoke and flames dancing in a clearing surrounded by trees.

"Before we go, try your best to block your minds," Jeno added.

Hector frowned. "You never taught me how."

"Just try to pull the energy around you like a curtain, like a wall around your head," Gertie said.

"Don't worry." Jeno clapped a hand on Hector's shoulder. "All you care about right now is saving your mother. No one will begrudge you that."

Hector squeezed Jeno's hand. "May the gods help us."

"Let's fly to those trees first," Gertie said. "So we can scope out the scene."

Gertie led them to the branches of a tall pine, where they hovered and watched. Down below, Hector's mother was already tied to the wooden post, exactly as Gertie had envisioned it!

In his animal form, Dionysus stood near the fire as the satyrs and Maenads encircled him in their dancing and pipe-playing. Some of the fifty or so vampires joined in the dance, but most hovered the perimeter as though they were keeping guard.

Gertie scoured the crowd and spotted Damien on Vladimir's back and Phoebe standing not far behind. Gertie tried to penetrate Phoebe's mind but found it powerfully blocked. Gertie suspected that Vladimir, who stood near the wooden post with a sword unsheathed and pointed at Dori, must have done something to prevent Phoebe from communicating with Gertie.

Hector handed his ukulele to Jeno. "Carry this for me? In case I need to use my sword?"

"Of course."

"Ready?" Hector asked.

Gertie and Jeno nodded and followed Hector toward the golden ram.

"Aha!" Dionysus cried, and the crowd grew silent and watchful. "The three little friends have returned. I hope that's Athena's shield you are holding? And what weapon have you, Jeno? A ukulele?"

Dionysus and his entourage laughed.

"We've brought the shield. Now free my mother!" Hector insisted.

"First things first," Dionysus replied. "I want to hear the vampire play a song. Don't you?" he asked the crowd.

The Maenads, satyrs, and vampires cheered and applauded.

When their noise died down, Jeno said, "This doesn't belong to me. It's Hector's."

"Then let the young demigod play!" Dionysus commanded.

Hector looked at his mother, who gave him a reassuring nod. Then he took the instrument from Jeno and played the same song he'd played at the Erechtheion the previous night (to hear Hector's song, go here: https://soundcloud.com/travispohler/alive-again):

I wish that I could feel alive again.
I don't know where, where I've been.

I've been away, away somewhere.

I surely wanted to stay,
But I went, and I died, I died that day.
One day ... I tried to stay.

I would have died either way,
And now my life has gone astray,
And I have felt Death's embrace,
And I would like Death to delay,
And I would like to live another day.
One day ... I want to stay.

I wish that I could feel alive again.
I don't know where, where I've been.
I've been away, away somewhere.

"Lovely performance," Dionysus said, and the crowd cheered.

Dionysus raised his hands to quiet the throng. "Don't we all wish we could feel alive? That very wish is what my nighttime dances are all about. We hope to feel free in the moment, to *experience* the moment."

Or to avoid things, Gertie thought.

"Free my mother," Hector insisted. "We brought you the shield."

"Vladimir, when the shield of Athena is in my hands, cut his mother loose," the golden ram commanded as the crowd quieted down again.

Carrying the shield, Gertie approached her father on shaky legs. Her feelings for him were mixed. She admired the fact that he wanted to help the vampires and was thankful that he had saved her from being executed by them, but she didn't like the way he was treating Hector's mother, or the way he was treating her. She was his daughter. Did he have no love for her?

As soon as she handed over the shield, Vladimir cut the ropes. Hector ran into his mother's arms, embracing her and kissing her cheeks.

But before they could leave, Dionysus roared, "I have been tricked! This shield is a fake! Seize them! Execute them!"

They'd been deceived by the golden snake?

In Gertie's vision, the snake had given her a jug of her father's wine, not a shield. Should she have recognized that as a sign?

In the next moment, Vladimir's blade cut through the air and across Dori's neck before Hector could unsheathe his sword. Then Vladimir seized Hector by the throat and drained him as the other vampires swarmed Dori's body.

Jeno and Gertie, forgotten in the blood lust and chaos, entered the crowd for Hector. Together they pushed and shoved their way to the center as the vampires were leaving the still bodies of Hector and his mother and the smashed ukulele and joining in another frenzied dance to the music of the satyrs. Hector had been completely drained and would die in a manner of minutes, just like his mother already had.

Jeno scooped Hector up in his arms, and then Gertie followed him away from the scene before anyone might notice they were gone, but the voice of Dionysus rang out above the throng of dancers and players just as they had lifted up into the smoky sky:

"You better return with the helm of invisibility, as originally planned, if you wish to live."

Dionysus hurled the fake shield of Athena at Gertie like a Frisbee. She caught it with two hands and said nothing in reply as they rushed with Hector's body toward Athens, once again leaving Phoebe and Damien behind.

C H A P T E R   T W E N T Y - O N E

Hector's Choice

Jeno led Gertie back to the barn, to the loft, where they'd been hiding out. He gingerly laid Hector down on the hay. Hector was awake, but his lips were blue, and he didn't seem to be all there.

"Why here?" Gertie asked, catching her breath as she dropped the shield on the floor beside them.

Jeno sat back on his heels. "We'll call the boy."

"Where's my mother?" Hector muttered through parched lips. "Is she…?"

"Gone," Gertie said. "I'm so sorry."

Hector stared back blankly, and then nodded.

"You will be too," Jeno said. "Unless you drink blood. Unless you turn into one of us."

Gertie heard the barn latch lift and the door creak open. The boy was coming. Jeno had called to him already.

"What?" Hector looked horrified. "You want me to become a vampire?"

"Oh, Hector." Gertie fought back tears. "It's either that or die. I'm so sorry."

Gertie heard the boy enter the barn and cross to the ladder, leading up to the loft.

"Just let me die. You two could, then you could…"

"Stop talking like that!" Gertie said. "I don't want you to die. I can't…"

"I don't want to live the rest of my life as a vampire," Hector said.

"Hector, please!" Gertie begged.

"It won't be permanent," Jeno said.

The boy made his way toward the top of the ladder. Jeno's power to mesmerize him without eye contact was made easier by the fact that the boy had already been bitten once—by Gertie.

"What do you mean it won't be permanent?" Hector asked. "Your father did this to me. Are you saying...?"

"I'm saying we will kill him," Jeno said. "Then you and Gertie will be free."

Air rushed from Gertie's throat as her mouth dropped open in surprise. "Jeno, I..."

Hector frowned. "Why would you do that?"

"Because I don't want you to die," Jeno said. "Not yet, anyway. You two are the only friends I've got."

Hector blinked back tears and clasped Jeno's hand like an arm wrestler before releasing it. "We'll figure this out together."

The boy reached the loft and stared dumbly at them.

Jeno climbed to his feet and said, "Very good. Now come, and we will make you strong."

The boy took several steps toward them and stopped a few feet away.

"You have to drink," Gertie whispered to Hector.

She climbed to her feet as Jeno beckoned the boy. The boy held out his wrist in obedience. She took it, pierced his flesh with her fangs, and offered the arm, spilling over with blood, to Hector.

Hector stared at the boy's bloody arm in horror. "I can't."

Recalling what Calandra had once told her, Gertie said, "It's always hard the first time." Then she added, "Don't think. Just drink."

Hector sat forward and, trembling, put his lips to the boy's wrist. After several seconds, his hesitance turned to enthusiasm, as he lapped up the blood already spurting from the wrist.

When half a pint had been taken from the boy, Gertie pulled the arm away from Hector and applied pressure to the wound. Both the boy and Hector were momentarily paralyzed as the vampire virus worked its way through their bloodstreams. Hector's mind was an open book as he felt the changes happening throughout his body. What was already a dense, muscular build became even more so. His hair, teeth, and nails, grew slightly longer. He had already been beautiful; now, he was magnificent.

Jeno took the boy out flying to reward him for his sacrifice while Gertie remained in the loft with Hector.

"Do you really think he can help us kill his father?" Hector asked her.

"I trust him," she said.

"I trust him, too. But maybe, when the time comes…"

I will not fail you, Jeno spoke to them telepathically. *You have my word.*

Hector lay back on the hay, covered his face, and wept.

Gertie curled up beside him, feeling numb and angry, and realizing, for maybe the first time in her life, that there was no one who would save her, no one who would protect her, and no one who could determine her fate but herself. It was the same for Hector and Jeno. If they wanted to ever find happiness in this world, there was no one, not even the gods, who would hand it over to them. They would have to figure it out, all on their own.

CHAPTER TWENTY-TWO

A Surprise at the Acropolis

I can't just lie here all night, thinking about her," Hector said to Gertie and Jeno once the boy had returned to his farmhouse. "Let's go tonight and do whatever it takes to get Athena's shield. We need that helm."

"You want to help the vampires after what they did?" Gertie asked.

"No," Hector said. "I want to make them think I'm helping, so I can get close enough to Vladimir. I want to kill him and rescue Damien and Phoebe. That's my plan. Are you with me?"

"I know you both hate the vampires right now," Jeno said. "But what happened tonight was caused by Dionysus. The vampires are still victims hoping for liberation. They do whatever their lord tells them to do."

"Including your father?" Hector asked.

Jeno rubbed his forehead, as though he were massaging away a headache. "Yes."

Gertie jumped to her feet. "Does this mean…?"

"No. I still want him dead," Jeno assured her. "He of all the vampires could have stood up to Dionysus, and he didn't. The other vampires are innocent."

"So what are you saying?" Hector asked.

Jeno stood up and looked out the window with his back to them. "If by some miracle we can rejoin the vampires, when we finally do turn on my father, let's try to keep the casualties to a minimum." He turned to face them. "Agreed?"

Gertie and Hector nodded.

"Of course," Hector said. "Now let's go catch a golden snake. I want to wring its neck."

Hector jumped past Jeno through the loft window and out into the night. Jeno looked back at Gertie before following. She grabbed the shield and took up the rear, not sure what Hector planned to do, but knowing he couldn't sit and think about his mother. He had to be doing something, even if it wasn't productive.

When they reached the place where the Erichtheion once stood, Hector shocked Gertie when he unzipped his pants and urinated as he sang:

I wish that I could feel alive again.
I don't know where, where I've been.
I've been away, away somewhere.

Hector was so full of anger, and Jeno had been right when he had said that the lyrics took on a new meaning from the mouth of a vampire.

The golden snake appeared before Hector had started the second verse of his song.

"What do you think you are doing, ssson of Hephaestusss?" Erich hissed angrily.

Hector tucked and zipped. "Your mean trick got my mother killed! She was a daughter to Apollo!"

"What mean trick, ssson of Hephaestusss? I did exactly asss you asssked."

Gertie stepped forward. "This shield is the fake, the one Hephaestus made."

"You are missstaken, little vampire," Erich said. "That isss the shield of Athena."

The three teens looked at one another, confused.

"Are you certain?" Jeno asked.

"Yesss. That shield bearsss the head of Medusssa."

"Why did Dionysus think it was a fake?" Gertie whispered to the others.

"Dionysusss? I thought you intended to hide the shield in the Underworld."

"We were threatened by the lord of the vampires," Hector explained. "He took the shield but thought it was a fake. He killed my mother because of it."

"He thought it was a fake becausssse he doesssn't know how to reanimate the head of Medusssa."

"How could he not know?" Gertie asked.

"Very few know," the snake said.

Hector dropped down on one knee. "I'm so sorry, my brother. Please accept my apology."

"Don't call me your brother, vampire! You may be a ssson of Hephaestusss, but no vampire isss a brother to me!"

Hector jumped to his feet yelling expletives Gertie could never have said herself, but Jeno took him by the elbow and said, "Let's get out of here. Now."

Gertie and Hector followed Jeno back to the sinkhole they had uncovered at the edge of the acropolis—their entrance to the Underworld.

"Don't forget about the Hydra," Jeno warned just before he dove in.

It wasn't easy to get Athena's shield though the narrow tunnels from the one sinkhole to the Hydra's, so the two boys helped her manipulate it though the openings. This slowed them down quite a bit, but eventually they emerged to the screeching cries of the dragon-headed monster.

Hector and Gertie followed Jeno's lead and flattened against the ceiling, waiting.

"It's okay, girl," Jeno said. "It's just me. Lord Hades is expecting us."

She cried out again but did not throw flames. Jeno took each of their arms and carefully guided them through the huge archway leading to the Phlegethon.

As they followed the river of fire to where it met the River Styx, Hector asked, "Do you ever get used to it?"

"Used to what?" Jeno asked, and then, after reading Hector's thoughts, said, "Ah. The insults. No, not me. It hurts every time. But that could just be me."

The three vampires walked along the river of fire, passing the stables after Jeno popped his head in to say hello to Swift and Sure, who neighed their replies. Gertie could sense how much Jeno missed the stallions and his old routine. He missed Calandra and their home beneath the acropolis. He missed his clock collection and his library and his family portraits. She wondered if he regretted ever meeting her.

Never, koureetsi mou, he said to her telepathically.

Hector's mind, on the other hand, was full of revenge. He was more angry than sad over his mother's death. He couldn't wait to personally destroy Jeno's father, now that Jeno supported it. He would help liberate the other vampires, but Vladimir would pay, and, if Hector could find allies among the gods—Hera, maybe—he wanted Dionysus to pay, too.

Gertie just wanted all of this to be over. Although she never again wished to be the girl that lived her life solely in books, she wanted to have the luxury of reading daily again, even if for just a few hours each night. And although she never wanted to go back to her old home in New York, she longed, more than anything, to be back with the Angelis family. They were home to her, they were family, and she missed them.

If she hoped to ever be accepted by them again, she had to bring Phoebe back. Damien was beyond saving, and she doubted anyone wanted him to go back to his tomb, buried alive. The only way to save Phoebe from the life of a vampire was to destroy Damien. Hector and Jeno must realize this, too.

Yes, Jeno said in her mind. *I'm not sure Hector has worked it out yet, but he will.*

Megaera appeared to them just before they reached the massive iron doors leading to the palace chambers of Hades and Persephone.

"Why are you here?" she asked.

"Your father asked us to bring him Athena's shield," Hector said. "He's expecting us."

"No," she said. "I don't think he is."

Then she faded from their sight, and they were left staring blankly at one another near the iron doors.

Before they knocked, the door opened, and Hecate poked out her head, her white and black hair falling over her shoulders.

"You've returned," she said, with disbelief. "You actually succeeded in stealing Athena's shield?"

"Let them in," Hades's voice rang eagerly from inside the palace chamber.

The three teens walked in to face the lord of the Underworld and his queen, who were gawking at them as though they were beings from another planet. Gertie stepped forward and presented the shield to Hades.

"The shield for the helm," she said.

CHAPTER TWENTY-THREE

The Helm of Invisibility

Since Hector had just lost his mother, Gertie and Jeno decided to give him the honor of wearing the helm as they stepped from Charon's raft and out into the bright day. As long as Hector held their hands, they were protected by the helm as well. It made them invisible and immune to light, just as Hades had said it would.

Even though she couldn't actually *feel* the sunlight on her skin, it was nevertheless incredible to Gertie to be walking around in the daylight again after nearly two months of living in darkness. Her delight was somewhat overshadowed by Jeno's, however, since, for him, it had been centuries. Tears streamed down his face, and his eyes were all but lost in his cheeks from his huge grin.

They flew above Athens, enjoying the sight of the city twinkling in Helios's rays, but, after about an hour of this, Gertie and Hector decided that the day belonged to Jeno. The three flew to Hector's house, and then Gertie and Hector remained behind so that Jeno could have the complete freedom of walking the streets in broad daylight beneath the protection of the helm.

Seeing Hector's bed again reminded Gertie of the visions she'd had of the two of them entwined in a passionate embrace. Her cheeks flushed as she tried to think of something else, but the only thing running through her mind was this thought: now that she might become human again, well, maybe now a future with Hector wasn't so impossible.

"You had a vision about us?" Hector asked, from where he'd been sitting at his desk texting the other demigods in his council.

"Get out of my head." She'd forgotten that he could read her mind, and, if he had, that meant Jeno probably had privy to her thoughts, too.

Jeno? she reached out.

He didn't reply.

"Why didn't you tell me?" Hector stood up and stuffed his phone in his pocket.

Even if she'd done a decent job guarding her mind from Jeno, Hector's was still an open book. There was no way this conversation was getting past Jeno, unless he was too absorbed in his daytime reveries.

"I don't want to talk about this," she said. "Not now."

"But you *do* have feelings for me," he said. "I knew it. You were just holding back because you didn't believe you'd ever be human again."

"For Jeno's sake, stop right now. Let him enjoy his sunshine."

"I love Jeno like a brother, but I just lost my mom. If there's any hope for you and me, well, I need to know. I need *something*, Gertie."

Jeno already knew of her feelings for Hector. Now that she thought about it, his willingness to kill his father to free her and Hector was probably his way of giving up, of setting her free of him.

Exactly, koureetsi mou.

"Oh, my God!" she sat on the bed and covered her face. Jeno *had* been listening. He *did* know. "Jeno."

"My name is Hector," Hector said with an edge of bitterness to his voice.

She looked up at him. Tears welled in his eyes. Whatever she chose to do, someone would get hurt. There was no good choice.

I give you my blessing, Jeno said to them telepathically. *I'm going to take a flight around the sunny side of the world and will return at dusk.*

Jeno, you're breaking my heart, Gertie replied. *I'm not ready to choose.*

Then I've just made the choice for you, he said.

Suddenly she could no longer read his thoughts or sense him. It was as if he had vanished. *Jeno?*

Nothing.

Gertie guarded her mind with the strongest shield she could muster as she gazed up at Hector. Although she felt guilty for Jeno's pain, the thought of loving Hector—fully and completely—filled her heart with joy.

"I need to teach you to block…"

Before she could finish her sentence, Hector hurled himself across the room to the bed, whisking her up in a feverish embrace.

"I can't wait another second," he said, just before he pressed his lips to hers.

He took her up in his arms and moved her to the center of the bed, so he could lie beside her and hold her close. They lay side by side with their arms around one another, kissing and kissing, and Gertie couldn't get enough. All the pent-up feelings she'd had for Hector for many months now were finally set free, and she was left wondering if this could really be possible, if she could really be loving Hector as he loved her back.

She had a vision of Jeno flying over Italy, of him weeping and thinking he had to be strong, had to keep up his guard. Then the vision was gone.

Poor Jeno!

Guarding her own mind, she allowed herself to realize that her feelings for Jeno had always been based on pity. They'd been part admiration and part pity, but her feelings for Hector hinged on desire—on a physical attraction that had been made stronger by her growing fondness for him.

Now she saw Jeno soaring over France. He faltered with his guard for a split second and then pulled it back up.

She had desired Jeno for the power he had given her with his bite before she had become a vampire, and once she had turned, that desire had faded away. It had been replaced by admiration, respect, and pity. Her love for him was real, but it was different than her love for Hector.

For, although she felt sorry for Hector for having just lost his mother, she didn't pity him the way she did Jeno. Jeno was more resigned about life, whereas Hector was a fighter. She could admire him without pity.

Her feelings for Hector overwhelmed her and took her breath away, and now, here she was, finally being held by him.

Gertie fell back on the bed, and Hector leaned over her with his elbows pressed into the pillow—one on each side of her head. He used his hands to cup her face as he gazed into her eyes.

"Tell me I'm not dreaming," he said.

"I'm not sure myself."

Jeno was flying over Ireland now, and his feelings of sadness and happiness were both so severe and equally present—she could sense them—that he wept and smiled at the same time, even as his guard went back up.

Hector rolled to his back and pulled her onto him as their legs entwined, just as she had seen it happen in her vision.

Hector and Gertie spent most of the day lying on his bed, talking and kissing and remembering and dreaming. For several hours, they were able to forget that they were vampires in the middle of a war. They were able to forget what they'd already lost and were able to dream of what they hoped would one day be.

Hector said he wanted to marry her one day, after they were human again, and have demigod babies with her. He said their children would probably have strong hidden talents.

Gertie laughed hysterically at this talk of marriage and babies. But after more of it from Hector, she joined in the game and said that maybe, by then, all would be forgiven by Mamá and Babá. Maybe Babá could even give her away, and Nikita and Phoebe could be her bridesmaids.

"Jeno and Klaus would be my groomsman," Hector said.

"Who would be your best man?"

"Jeno for sure. I love Klaus, but I've never had a friend like Jeno."

At some point, they each took a shower and changed into fresh clothes, and as they sat on the sofa in his room flipping through the channels on the television, they began to feel their craving for blood. When night fell, they became worried about Jeno.

"What do you think is keeping him?" Hector asked.

Gertie reached out with her mind but couldn't sense him. "I don't know."

Fear swept through Hector's mind. It was brief and he dismissed it, but she had caught it, nonetheless. Hector had wondered if it was possible that Jeno might have betrayed them. Maybe he had taken the helm to the vampires without them.

But on the heels of that thought came another: Jeno would never do that. They both knew him well enough to feel confident that he wouldn't betray them.

Could something have happened to him?

"If he doesn't get here soon, I'm going to be really worried," Gertie said.

"Me, too."

<u>CHAPTER TWENTY-FOUR</u>

The Summons

At midnight, Gertie and Hector walked the streets of downtown Athens near Omonoia Square, searching for Jeno's contacts.

"I really hope he's okay," Gertie said again.

"Let's just stick with the plan."

The plan was that as soon as they had fed, they would look for Jeno at the vampire camps—first at Mt. Kithairon, then at Alexander, and, finally, at the labyrinth in Knossos. They didn't think he had betrayed them, but they did fear he'd been captured and taken prisoner.

Gertie led Hector into one of her and Jeno's regular stops—the very first bar Jeno had ever taken her to. She scanned the smoky room for Aggie, a bubbly woman in her thirties who was addicted to the vampire virus, but was disappointed not to see her among the patrons. Then she picked her way through the crowd toward the bar, looking for Old Man Mikos, another addict. She and Jeno had fed on him recently—too recently—but she could sense Hector's feelings of panic as his need for blood escalated. Maybe the old man could afford to lose more than a pint that month.

When she reached the bar, she found his usual stool occupied by someone else. Two strikes.

"I'm sorry," she said to Hector. "Let's get out of here."

"I feel like I could easily suck the blood of the next human who bumps into me," he murmured as he followed her toward the door.

Just then, a woman did bump into Hector, and his mouth opened and exposed his fangs in an automatic gesture that mortified him. The woman winced and gasped in terror as he rushed past Gertie from the bar and out onto the sidewalk.

Gertie quickly caught up to him. "Are you okay?"

"No. I won't be okay until Vladimir is destroyed."

She read his thoughts of helplessness. He'd never felt so out of control and couldn't wait to be human again.

"It's hard being a victim," she said.

"That doesn't make me feel any better, Gertie."

She rubbed her hand across his back and said, "I know another place. Come on."

A few blocks down, they entered a café that was about to close up for the night. There were no customers, only a clerk behind the counter wiping down his machines.

"Good evening, Pedro," Gertie said. "Is this a good time for you?"

The man—young, in his twenties—turned to face her, glanced at Hector, and asked, "Where's Jeno?"

"I'm not sure. I'm actually a little worried about him. This is my friend, Hector. He's Jeno's friend, too."

Pedro nodded, but the look of suspicion did not leave his face. "I serve only Jeno."

"Hector is new and just needs something to hold him over until he can really feed."

"I serve only Jeno." Pedro draped his rag across the sink and wiped his hands on his apron. "I need to close up. Excuse me."

Pedro disappeared into the back room.

Strike three.

"Now what?" Hector asked.

She could tell he was at the point when it hurts, when the pain begins to drive you mad. She knew that feeling all too well.

"Come on," she said, leading him from the café.

Out on the street, she spotted the three older women who had first accosted her when she was new to Athens. They were leading some students into an alley. As Gertie looked more closely at the students, she recognized them from four weeks ago. They were the same five who had lost their friend, Alyssa.

Gertie realized that the power to mesmerize a victim increased once you'd bit them. This explained how Jeno was able to mesmerize the boy from the barn without making eye contact.

Just as they had that tragic night four weeks ago, the three boys and two girls stood with their backs against the building, waiting for their supposed elixir. The three vampires stepped in front of the three boys, leaving the two girls on the end for last.

"This way," Gertie said.

As the older vampires sank their fangs into the three boys, Gertie and Hector pranced on the two waiting girls.

The vampire closest to them hissed and cried, "Get away!"

Gertie and Hector kept drinking and had nearly consumed a pint each when the three women attacked, scratching and biting and kicking. Gertie and Hector broke away and flew off toward Mt. Kithairon, but not without feeling utterly ashamed.

Hector was silent during the flight away from Athens. His mind, however, was at war with itself. He couldn't believe what he'd just done, and yet his body was rejoicing at the new blood pumping through his veins. He couldn't wait to kill Vladimir. The sooner, the better.

Gertie wished she could think of something to say.

There was no bonfire glowing from Mt. Kithairon, nor was there any sign of a dance. Except for animals and insects, the mountainside was quiet.

When they landed at the clearing where Hector's mother had been killed, Hector fell to his knees.

"I don't know what I expected to find," he murmured.

Gertie landed beside him. "I'm so sorry."

"Why didn't Apollo help her? She was his daughter. Didn't he care about her?"

"Parents can suck sometimes."

He shook his head. "I wonder what they did with her body."

Gertie shielded her mind because it was more than likely that the Maenads had consumed Dori. If they hadn't, then the animals that lived in this area probably had. It was better that Hector hadn't drawn the same conclusions. He was imaging a funeral pyre. She hoped, for his sake, he was right.

She squeezed his shoulder. "Do you need a few minutes?"

"No. I want vengeance."

"Then let's go."

As they were about to take off, they saw someone flying toward them—someone small, whose mind was heavily guarded.

It was Phoebe!

They lifted up and met her in the sky.

Gertie embraced her. "Phoebe! I'm so happy to see you!"

Hector was next. "Thank the gods you're safe."

"What are you doing here?" Gertie asked.

"Lord Vladimir ordered me to bring you to the labyrinth," she said.

"What makes him think we'll follow his orders?" Hector asked.

"Because he's got Jeno," she said. "And if you don't show up, Vladimir will kill him."

Gertie and Hector exchanged glances.

"Okay," Gertie said. "We'll go with you."

"Hold on," Hector said. "I have an idea."

"If we don't hurry, more vampires will come," Phoebe warned.

Hector jumped into the air. "Then let's go. But I need to make a stop along the way."

As Gertie flew beside Hector, she was able to read his plan from his thoughts. He wanted to return Phoebe to the Angelis family before continuing on to the labyrinth.

They can't see her like this, Gertie said to him telepathically, unsure if Phoebe was capable of reading Gertie's thought. Perhaps the strong wall around her mind worked both ways. It must, or the little girl would be reacting to Hector's thoughts.

We'll put her in Damien's tomb, where she'll be safe, Hector explained.

The tomb? That will scare the crap out of her.

That way she won't have to be there when we kill Damien, Hector said telepathically.

So Hector *had* worked it out that Damien had to be killed.

That way she'll be safe, Hector added.

Maybe he was right.

As they neared Athens, Hector took out his phone and sent a text. By checking his mind, Gertie discovered that he was alerting demigods in the area that Phoebe would need protection at the Angelis apartment building, just in case the other vampires learned of their plan.

When Phoebe realized the new direction they had taken, she looked at Gertie with wide eyes. "Lord Vladimir said he would kill my family if I went anywhere near my home."

Hector grabbed Phoebe, pinning her arms to her sides as they continued to descend toward the city. "Listen to me. This is for your own protection. I'm going to save you, make you human again."

"But that means…"

"Your parents have already lost Damien," Hector said. "They won't be able to handle losing you, too. Let me do this for them."

"And for Klaus and Nikita," Gertie added. "They all miss you so much."

"But they'll be killed!" Phoebe cried, as she squirmed against Hector's grip.

"My council of demigods is already on its way to guard them," Hector said, just before they flew into an open window and headed for the basement stairs.

"Where are you taking me?" Phoebe asked.

"Shh," Gertie said. "We can't let your parents see you in this condition. It will traumatize them."

"We want you to hide in here," Hector said as he sat her down in Damien's tomb.

The tomb was small, but it was large enough for Phoebe.

Tears fell from the little girl's round brown eyes. "I'm scared. Please take me with you."

"Do this for your parents," Gertie begged.

At last, Phoebe nodded and lay down in the tomb willingly.

"I'm going to lock you in so no one can get to you," Hector said. "Don't be frightened. Just go to sleep."

Gertie knew that no amount of words could prevent Phoebe from being scared out of her mind. Being locked in a tomb had to be one of the worst things a person could ever experience, but it really was the surest way they could keep her safe without horrifying her family.

Before they shut the lid, Gertie leaned in and kissed Phoebe's cheek. "We'll be back as soon as we can."

<u>CHAPTER TWENTY-FIVE</u>

Prison Shock

It was almost dawn when they reached Knossos. Gertie quickly led Hector down into the caves. Two vampires were standing guard.

"Where's the little one?" one of them asked.

Hector was an open book, so lying would do no good.

"She went home," Gertie said. "And she's heavily guarded by a council of demigods."

"Where's Jeno?" Hector asked.

"Inside," the guard replied. "Follow me."

On the floor of the cave was a red wire, which the guard followed into the labyrinth. The tunnels twisted and turned and split away from another, and the wire seemed to be leading them deeper and deeper underground. They passed a few rooms along the way, and even though they had wooden doors, Gertie could see through them to the prisoners inside. She recognized the demigod she had once mistaken for Hector. There were other prisoners, too, and a quick check of their minds confirmed they were all demigods. Jeno must be in one of these rooms, too.

Poor Jeno.

She wondered how long he'd been a prisoner here and how he'd been captured, especially since he had the invisibility of the helm. He must have taken it off before he was discovered. But why would he do that?

At last, the vampire guard stopped in front of a door where another vampire stood watch.

"In there," he said, unlocking the door.

Gertie and Hector stepped inside.

As soon as they'd entered, the vampire slammed the door behind them and secured the lock. They had walked directly into a trap. Jeno was nowhere in sight.

They rushed the door and pounded their fists against it.

"Wait a minute!" Hector shouted.

"Where's Jeno?" Gertie hollered out. "Please!"

When a few minutes passed, and they got no reply, Gertie said to Hector, "I can't get a read on Jeno. Can you?"

"I get nothing. What do you think they're planning to do?"

"I can't get inside anyone's mind—not anyone who seems to know why we're here or what's going on with Jeno."

Hector took her in his arms. "I'm so sorry that your first trip to Athens has been such a bummer."

Gertie laughed, and so did Hector. They were both feeling so helpless and frightened, and laughter was all they had left.

"My life already sucked before," she said. "At least here I found a real family and true best friends."

"And met your future husband," he said with a wink.

"There's that." She smiled back. Then she murmured, "God, I hope Jeno's okay. What if they've already killed him?"

"I've been praying to Hera and Hephaestus," Hector said, holding her more tightly. "We can't give up hope."

"I'm not holding my breath for their help," she said. "No disrespect to your father, but parents suck. Most of them care for themselves more than anything and don't mind throwing their own kids under the bus."

"My mom wasn't like that."

"I know." She kissed him. "I'm sorry. And neither are Nikita's parents. I miss them both so much."

He turned away to pace. "My mom *was* gone a lot. She was always at the hospital. And I guess I resented that, even though she was there helping others. Sometimes it seemed like she cared more about her duties than she did me."

"I'm sorry. I know she loved you. That day you went missing, she found me under the guestroom bed. I could read her thoughts. She was terrified. If she didn't find you, she was going to go see Apollo's oracle."

"Really?"

"Really. And while I was reading her thoughts, I saw her inner conflict."

"What do you mean?"

"She felt guilty. She justified it by telling herself that she'd been there for you when you were little, when no one else was."

"That's true. She was."

"But once you became independent, she didn't think you needed her as much."

"I didn't need her as much. But I still needed her *some*."

"She didn't know how you felt."

He raked a hand through his hair. "I'm not exaggerating when I say she was rarely there. She'd have dinner with me maybe once a week. Three or four times a week, she'd leave me breakfast on the stove in the morning." Tears formed in his eyes but didn't fall. "I miss her so much. I missed her when she was alive. And I miss her even more now."

Gertie wrapped her arms around his waist and pressed her cheek against his chest. She didn't say anything. She just held him and wept.

Sometime later, they heard a noise at the door. Vladimir stood on the other side with Damien still clinging to his back. Gertie and Hector wiped their eyes and waited.

Without opening the door, Vladimir said, "I'm sorry to be the one to tell you this, but Jeno told me everything. He told me about your plan to destroy me. He told me that you never intended to help with our uprising."

"What?" Gertie cried, rushing to the door. "That's not true."

"Are you calling my son a liar?"

Damien gave her a maniacal smile.

"No," Gertie said angrily. "I'm calling *you* a liar. Jeno would never say that. And you can read my mind, if you don't believe me."

"Your thoughts prove your intent to harm me."

"True. After what you did to Hector and his mom, I want you dead. But I support the vampires. I'm no traitor to *them*. *You're* the traitor, for turning your back on your own son!"

"My son has been forgiven for his crimes against me and our people," Vladimir said. "We've been reconciled."

"Then let us see him," Hector said. "Prove to us he's still alive."

"You think you have the power to make demands of me, young demigod? I don't take orders from you."

"You think you're in charge?" Gertie taunted. "Apparently, my daddy's running things. You better watch out how you treat me. We want to see Jeno now!"

"You're daddy?" Vladimir arched a brow.

"Why do you think Dionysus protected me from you? He's my father."

"That's a good joke," Vladimir said. "Very funny."

"Why don't you ask him yourself?" Hector challenged.

"It doesn't matter. The gods don't care about their children. If they did, I would have no prisoners, and as you saw on your way through, I have at least a dozen. I made a mistake when I thought I could use them as leverage. The helm is much better. Thank you for that."

That statement caught Gertie off guard, because, unfortunately, it was true.

"I'm glad to hear you support the uprising," Vladimir continued. "But I can't afford to keep you alive, now that I know about your vendetta against me. I'll execute you tonight, when the others are able to return. They won't want to miss it."

"We want to see Jeno!" Gertie said. "If you're going to kill us anyway, what does it matter if we see him?"

"Fine. But don't be too hard on him for selling you out. He was only doing his duty."

Vladimir turned and walked away with Damien clinging to his back.

Gertie turned to Hector. "I don't believe him."

"Neither do I. He's toying with us, for some reason. Maybe he's trying to pit us against one another."

"Jeno would never sell us out."

"I agree."

"You're wrong," Jeno said from beyond the door.

"Jeno? Are you okay?" Gertie asked.

"I'm fine."

"How did they capture you?" Hector said. "How could they when you had the helm?"

"I wasn't captured," Jeno said.

Gertie's throat tightened as all the air left her body. "What did you say?"

"I said I wasn't captured," he repeated. "I came willingly to warn my father and to deliver the helm."

"You did what?" Hector asked.

"I lied to you," Jeno said.

Gertie dropped to her knees, completely shocked. She never saw this coming.

Hector seemed equally speechless, but after several surreal seconds, he asked, "How could you? You gave us your word!"

"This is war," Jeno said. "I grew to care for you, but my devotion to my father is greater."

Gertie felt the blood leave her face. She couldn't speak. Couldn't breathe.

"So you were lying to us?" Hector asked.

"Yes."

"Wait," Hector shook his head. "From the very beginning? Or did you change your mind later?"

"What does it matter?"

Hector raked his hand through his hair. "It matters."

"From the very beginning."

Gertie burst into tears—ugly sobs that caused her whole body to convulse. She wailed, too. She didn't care. Her heart was utterly broken, and she didn't care. What was there left to care about? If your own parents and your own friends can turn on you, why go on?

She wished she had never come to Athens. Her life may have sucked, but at least *back then* she could get lost in a book. There was no recovering from this. Jeno's betrayal was the final straw. She no longer cared to live.

Hector looked down at her, horrified. "No, Gertie. You still have *me*."

I'm sorry, Hector, but I'm done. How can I ever trust anyone again after this?

"You bastard!" Hector growled at Jeno. "Here I thought you were making a noble sacrifice. But you knew all along, didn't you? You meant to crush us both!"

"Please, Hector," Gertie murmured near the ground. "Just stop."

He knelt beside her. "And what about Phoebe, hmm? Do we just leave her there, locked inside that tomb?"

Gertie had been so shocked by Jeno's betrayal that she had forgotten about Phoebe. Would the other demigods kill her after she and Hector were destroyed?

Vladimir came up behind Jeno and said, "Don't worry. We know where she is. We'll bring her back where she belongs."

CHAPTER TWENTY-SIX

A Final Betrayal

After Hector and Gertie were left alone, they huddled together on the floor with their backs propped against the wall of their cell. Gertie made it clear that she didn't want to talk, so Hector just held her quietly and ran his fingers through her hair, again and again, until she fell asleep.

She awoke to the sound of vampire guards approaching. The door was opened, and two guards entered. Each held iron cuffs. The taller one used his to bind Hector's wrists behind his back. The shorter one did the same to Gertie.

Gertie tried to make eye contact with the vampire, but he wouldn't look at her.

"Read my mind," she said. "You'll see I want to help the vampires. It's Vladimir I'm against."

The taller vampire turned to her and said, "The destruction of Vladimir would lead to our own. He's our maker. If you're against him, you're against us."

She looked over their young faces. They didn't appear much older than Jeno. Vladimir probably turned them when he was still a new vampire and unable to control his cravings. These boys didn't deserve to die any more than she and Hector did. They were victims.

"It's too late for a change of heart," the older one added. "Come with us. We're taking you to Mount Kithairon for your execution."

They followed the red wire from the depths of the labyrinth. On the way, Gertie prayed to Asterion, the Minotaur, and Ariadne for help. They'd made friends the first time Gertie had been taken prisoner there, and maybe, somehow, some way, they could help her and Hector now.

As they reached the exit, the vampire who had cuffed her grabbed her by the arm and lifted her up into the sky, but before they were more than a few feet in the air, an enormous force hurled into her, forcing her against Hector and the other vampires. They flew backwards until they hit against the side of the palace ruins and landed in a heap.

Gertie got the wind knocked out of her and gasped for air as someone scooped her up and carried her off. It was Ariadne, and behind them, running at full speed, was Asterion with Hector draped across one shoulder. Their rescuers ran across the land with the palace ruins at their backs, headed away from the sea. They darted on the outskirts of the town and into a forest. After another mile of weaving through the trees, their rescuers stopped to catch their breath and put them down.

"Oh my gosh!" Gertie cried. "Thank you! Thank you so much!"

"We wanted to help you earlier," Ariadne said in between breaths. "But we couldn't locate you until you started praying."

Gertie smiled and shook her head. "Sounds like I should have started sooner."

"You must be Hector," the Minotaur said. "I'm Asterion, and this is my sister, Ariadne. It's great to finally meet you."

"I'd shake your hand, but I'm a bit tied up." Hector gave his charming smile.

"I'm sorry, we don't have the key." Ariadne shrugged. "But maybe if we pray to Hephaestus, he'll forge one for us."

A deep voice sounded from the nearby woods. "There won't be time for that."

Ariadne's eyes widened, and then she frowned. "Dionysus."

He stepped from the trees into their line of vision and stood before them in his true form. He looked exactly as he had appeared to Gertie in her vision, the night he'd told her that only the Fates see the certain future. Gertie gasped when she sensed Jeno behind him. He had three other vampires with him.

"There's a party going on at Kithairon," Dionysus said. "And everyone's waiting on the guests of honor."

"Why must you do this?" Ariadne asked. "If you love me, you'll let these prisoners go."

"They mean to destroy my most powerful commander," Dionysus replied. "And that will wipe out several more innocent people. I need them for the uprising."

"You don't care about the vampires," Gertie said. "You don't care about anyone but yourself."

Dionysus glanced back at the vampires gathered behind him. "If I didn't care about them, why would I fight for them?"

"You want any reason to oppose the other gods," she said. *"That's why you take up the cause of the disenfranchised."*

"You need to learn to show more respect when addressing a god," he roared. Then to the vampires behind him, he said, "Seize them!"

Jeno flew up to Gertie and grabbed her arm as another vampire came up on the other side of her. She tried to speak to him telepathically, asking him how he could do this to her, but his mind was heavily guarded. He briefly met her eyes and turned away, ignoring her as they lifted up into the star-filled sky.

Hector was grabbed by two other vampires and they followed, and then the entire flight toward Mount Kithairon was a blur. Gertie had lost her fighting spirit. Ariadne and Asterion had given her hope, but it had been destroyed the moment Jeno had shown up to deliver her and Hector to his father.

The bonfire was already aflame in the clearing on the mountainside. Maenads and satyrs gathered with the rest of the army of vampires, Vladimir among them standing near two wooden posts. Damien clung to

Vladimir's back and smiled maniacally as Hector and Gertie were tied to the posts. Vladimir drew his sword.

Dionysus also appeared in the form of a golden ram. Gertie wished she could do something to teach him a lesson. Gods shouldn't treat their people the way he treated them, and fathers shouldn't treat their daughters the way he treated her. She closed her eyes and prayed to Hera, begging her to do something to stop him.

Dionysus stepped toward the center near Vladimir and said, "Tonight we will celebrate the execution of two enemies of our cause. These two demigods planned to betray us, and tonight we remind one another that we are a force that will not be stopped."

The crowd exploded in cheers and applause.

As the golden ram spoke again, the crowd quieted down. "After this, we will use the helm to negotiate with the gods on Mount Olympus."

The crowd erupted with more cheering.

"We have Jeno to thank for this," Dionysus added.

As the crowd applauded Jeno, he stood beside his father but did not look at Gertie. She hoped to appeal to him one more time, but he gave her no chance.

"*We* got the helm!" Hector shouted. "Jeno had help! He couldn't have done it without us!"

"We thank you for your contribution," Vladimir said as he held up the sword.

"You promised this pleasure to me," Jeno said to his father.

Gertie blanched. Jeno wanted to personally kill them? Tears rushed to her eyes. How could she have been so easily fooled by him? He wasn't at all the person she believed him to be, because *that* person would never, could never say such a thing.

Vladimir handed the sword over to his son.

Jeno took the sword and held the end of the blade at Hector's throat. "You think you know someone well until the pressures of war bring out his true characteristics. You think someone loves you and is devoted to you until a cause comes along that drives him mad with obsession."

Wait a minute, Gertie thought. *What was Jeno saying?*

Suddenly, in a movement so swift and so sure that it almost could not be seen with the naked eye, Jeno turned and cut the blade across the necks of Vladimir and Damien. Both heads fell near Gertie's feet. Instantly, at least a third of the vampires disintegrated into dust and the others, taken by surprise, looked around in shock.

The shock of the others gave Jeno the time he needed to grab Hector and Gertie from the wooden posts and lift into the air at a speed approaching that of light. He held them each by an arm and soared away from Crete.

Gertie didn't know where they were headed, but it didn't matter. Her face split in half with the biggest smile of her life. Jeno hadn't betrayed them.

"That couldn't have been easy, man," Hector said. "I'm sorry for your loss."

"Thank you," Jeno said. "I'm sorry I couldn't tell you what I was up to. Your mind is an open book. Vladimir would have seen right through it."

"I get it," Hector said.

"When did you think it up?" Gertie asked as they flew over France.

"As soon as we got the helm from Hades. I realized that if we delivered it together, Vladimir would kill all three of us. But if I proved my loyalty to him by appearing to betray you, I could get close to him. I made sure he promised to let me be the one to execute you."

"Yeah, that was pretty key," Hector said with a smile. "Pretty brilliant, too."

Gertie suddenly remembered Phoebe. "She'll be human now, right? But trapped in that tomb!"

"Don't worry," Jeno assured her. "We're headed there now."

He plunged down toward Athens, toward the Angelis apartment building. Gertie filled with excitement. She couldn't wait to be reunited with the people she loved. She was so glad, so glad to be human again and couldn't wait to start living the life she was meant to lead.

"I still want to fight with you," Gertie said to Jeno. "I want to help the vampires, okay?"

"Me, too," Hector said. "I'll convince my council as well. We *will* liberate your people. Together."

They reached the basement of the Angelis apartment building where Hector pulled the switch on the light before they unlocked the chains around Phoebe's tomb. When they lifted the lid, she sat up, coughing.

"Oh my gods! I thought you were never coming!" She climbed from the tomb full of smiles.

A flurry of footsteps could be heard approaching the basement door, and soon Mamá's head could be seen peaking from the doorway above.

"Jeno? Are you here?"

"Yes, Marta," Jeno said. "I called you down here because I have a surprise for you. But first, call the others."

"Tell me now, Jeno!" Mamá insisted. "Do you have my babies?"

"Damien was beyond saving," Jeno said.

"Phoebe? Gertie? And Hector?" she asked.

Gertie's eyes filled with tears at the sound of her name on Mamá's lips. Hector squeezed her hand.

"Come see for yourself after you call down the rest of your family," Jeno said.

Mamá screamed at the top of her lungs rather than leave the basement. She must have left her apartment door open, because Gertie heard Nikita yelling back at her.

"What is it, Mamá?"

Gertie, Hector, and Phoebe laughed.

"Come down here now! Bring Babá and Klaus! Hurry! Oh, please hurry!"

When she heard the rest of them descending the steps, Mamá could wait no longer. She burst down into the basement, her face full of tears, and her eyes hidden by her smiling cheeks. Phoebe ran into her mother's outstretched arms. Mamá kissed her all over her cheeks and the top of her head.

Nikita came bounding down the steps and squealed with glee at the site of everyone gathered below.

Klaus was on her heels. "Phoebe!"

Babá, who took the rear, complained that they were all clogging the steps. "Go down! Go down!"

Jeno stood on the sidelines as the family and friends reunited with one another.

"Mamá and Babá!" Phoebe cried.

"What?" Mamá froze. "You can talk?"

Babá jumped so high that he hit his head on a wooden beam, but he laughed and cried, "Phoebe can talk!"

Nikita and Klaus jumped up and down with excitement, too, and there was more hugging and exclaiming with joy.

But in the middle of all the rejoicing, Gertie realized something. While Hector and Phoebe had already turned into humans again, she remained a vampire.

She met Jeno's shocked gaze across the room, for he had heard her thoughts, and they had brought her unchanged form to his attention, too.

What does this mean? she asked him telepathically as Nikita hugged her neck.

He didn't answer for many seconds as Klaus and then Babá and, finally, Mamá embraced her.

Finally he said, *It means you are mine. It means I made you, not my father.*

Hector noticed her worried expression from across the room. As he made his way toward her, she wondered how she could break the news to him. She wouldn't become human after all.

His future with her was no longer possible.

THE END

Thank you for reading my story. If you enjoyed it, please consider leaving a review. Reviews help other readers to find my books, which helps me.

Please enjoy this excerpt from the next book, *Vampire Ascension*.

CHAPTER ONE

Not Again

Mamá gasped. "Gertoula?"

The basement of the Angelis's apartment building became very quiet. The joyful noises from their family reunion, from the realization that Phoebe could speak and that Gertie and Hector were safe, and from the blissful feeling of being in one another's arms again came to a halt the moment Mamá noticed that Gertie had not changed.

Gertie was still grappling with it, too. She was trying to convince herself that she was okay. Being human again wasn't necessary to her happiness. She could deal with it. But when she looked into Mamá's horrified eyes, her knees gave out, and she fell to the floor.

"Gertie!"

When was the last time she had fed?

Both Hector and Jeno rushed to her aid, one on each side of her. They looked down at her, their heads nearly touching as the room spun behind them.

"What's happening to her?" Hector asked Jeno. "Why is she still a vampire?"

Nikita and Klaus knelt on the floor beside Hector.

"Does she need a doctor?" Nikita asked. "Jeno, can't you help her? Hector, use your healing powers. Somebody do something!"

"I'm okay." Gertie squeezed Nikita's hand. "Seriously."

Are you going to tell them or should I? Jeno asked her telepathically.

Neither of us needs to say anything. Gertie saw no reason to alert everyone that Jeno was responsible for her becoming a vampire—that Jeno would be the one who'd have to die if she were to ever be human again. What good would it do to tell people that? There was no way she'd ever even consider taking Jeno's life to save her own.

Jeno arched a brow, but she ignored it and sat up.

Before she could say another word, Mamá knelt beside her, too, and said, "You are a part of this family, Gertoula. I won't have you leave us again. No matter what."

Gertie glanced across the room at Babá, who swallowed hard and nodded. "Mamá is right. We were wrong to make you leave. We were afraid—are still afraid—but we will be brave this time."

Holding back tears, Gertie tried to give Babá a smile, but her mouth made more of a frown. As Nikita hugged her, the hairs on the back of Gertie's neck prickled.

Jeno stood up and said to Hector. "They're coming. We need to be ready to fight."

"I'll call for backup." Hector took out his phone and sent a text. Then he opened one of the closet doors and found a sword and scabbard. His thoughts told Gertie that he had stashed them there for emergencies. "Klaus, take your family upstairs."

"Do you have another one of those swords?" Klaus asked.

"No. Why?"

"I want to fight, too," he said.

"You may have to." Jeno grabbed a crowbar from the floor. "They're here."

Babá gathered Nikita and Phoebe in his arms. "Come, Marta. Hide in here."

Just as he opened one of the basement closet doors, Phoebe screamed.

From the top of the stairs, six vampires flew into the room like a flock of giant birds. Gertie's super-human reflexes kicked into gear as she spun around, fists swinging.

Hector drew his sword and decapitated one of the intruders. Jeno clutched the crowbar and drove it, like a wooden stake, through the heart of another. Gertie had no weapon but herself. And Klaus was even worse off, because he had no weapon *and* no extra-human strength. From the corner of her eye, she saw him being pinned against the wall. Euripides stretched open his mouth, fangs protracted.

"No!" Gertie screamed.

Mamá and Nikita also screamed as Babá charged Euripides—like he was any match against a vampire. Euripides tossed him across the room like a rag doll. Gertie shoved the one fighting her and scrambled to Klaus's aid, but the other vampire grabbed her by the ankles and pulled her away. Hector decapitated the one holding her and set her free just as another leapt onto Hector's back and stabbed his fangs in Hector's neck. Gertie pulled the attacker off Hector and hissed as she fought with him. They threw one another against the wall, the ceiling, the floor.

Then Jeno had her attacker by the throat and pinned against the wall. He drove the bloody crowbar through the vampire's chest before turning to Gertie.

"Klaus!" she cried.

Only two vampires remained: Euripides had completely drained Klaus and was holding him like a lover. The other vampire, a female, crouched before them, guarding her clan leader from Hector and Babá, who charged them repeatedly.

Mamá lunged forward. "Don't you dare take another one of my children!" She stood, trembling, before Euripides and his guard. "Take me instead!"

"Mamá, no!" Nikita cried.

Eyes dark and fierce, Euripides stretched open his mouth, his fangs at the ready, but as he went to bite Mamá, Gertie flew in between the two and took the bite in her arm.

Although Gertie couldn't destroy Euripides, her stunt was enough of a distraction for Jeno to move in past the guard, grab the languid Klaus, and flee the basement. Hector, who'd been infected with the virus, flew up and swung his blade toward the guard, but she ducked and followed Euripides up the basement stairs. They went after Jeno and Klaus, as Jeno knew they would.

Hector and Gertie followed, leaving the rest of the Angelis family behind.

Gertie felt the sting of dawn coming as she and Hector found Jeno in the air above Athens shouting at Euripides.

"I'm on your side, you idiot!" Jeno yelled. "My enemy was my father, not you! I was going to come back, to fight with you. And with Lord Hades!"

And I loved my father, but he was wrong, Jeno's thoughts continued.

Gertie's stomach tied into a knot.

"I will never trust you!" Euripides hollered back. "I'll never believe another word you say."

"You need our help," Jeno shouted. "So few of us remain."

"We plan to remedy that tonight," Euripides said. "Now hand over what's mine."

Gertie sensed he meant Klaus.

"Klaus will never be yours!" Gertie screamed. "Read my mind. Jeno speaks the truth. We always intended to help free the vampires."

"Why should I trust a girl who can't even decide which boy she loves?" Euripides sneered. "You and Jeno are better to me dead than alive! Next time, I will kill you myself!"

Hector, who hovered beside her, turned beet red. "Don't talk to her like that!"

"Dawn's breaking," Euripides said. "So you can have the boy for now. But he's mine, and I will be calling for him!" He pointed to Hector. "And you better watch your back. I'm coming for you next!"

The first rays of the sun broke through and stung. Gertie resisted crying out as Euripides and his guard vanished, and she followed the others back to the Angelis's basement.

It took a moment to recover from the stinging burn of her flesh as she sat on the floor between Hector and Jeno, with Klaus barely conscious beside them.

The dawn almost did me in, Jeno said to her telepathically. *I don't think I have much blood left in my body.*

"Klaus!" Mamá rushed to him.

He was weak but awake. "I'm okay."

Two men and a woman the same age as Mamá and Babá descended the stairs.

One of them men extended his hand toward Hector. "Looks like we're too late."

Hector grabbed the man's hand and climbed to his feet. "They'll come back."

"What do we do about Klaus?" Mamá cried with her arms around her son.

Babá joined her. "Is he dying?"

"I'm okay," Klaus insisted again.

"We can turn him," Jeno suggested.

"No!" Babá cried. "Not again. Not another one of my sons. One suffered too long already."

"I don't want to be a tramp," Klaus growled. "If I'm going to die, just let me die."

"This is different," Hector said.

"You support this?" the demigod who had helped Hector up asked him. "What about the law?"

"You have a lot to learn," Hector said without arrogance.

The man gave Hector a look of disapproval.

Gertie climbed to her feet. "If we kill Euripides, Klaus will be restored."

"And we *will* kill him," Jeno said.

"Promise me!" Mamá cried. "Promise me he won't stay a vampire!"

"He speaks the truth," Phoebe said. "It happened to me. We can save Klaus. You've got to trust them, Mamá. Please, Klaus. Let them turn you."

Klaus stared at Phoebe. After a moment, he nodded wordlessly.

Mamá hugged Klaus again before releasing him as tears streamed down her face.

Babá took her in his arms and said to Jeno, "Do what you have to do to save our son."

CHAPTER TWO

Klaus

The three demigods who'd responded to Hector's text promised to return at dusk and station themselves around the building, even though Gertie could tell they had very mixed feelings about allowing Klaus to be turned into a vampire.

"Let's go upstairs," Mamá said once the other demigods had left. "Where we can think."

"The light hurts them," Phoebe said.

"We can close the blinds," Nikita offered. "Won't that work?"

Jeno nodded. "Go ahead. But hurry. Your brother doesn't have much time."

Nikita rushed up the stairs with Phoebe right behind her.

Hector gathered Klaus in his arms, and once Nikita hollered down that they had closed all the blinds, he led the way upstairs to the Angelis apartment. The window in the stairwell had no covering, so the ascent burned, but once they were in the apartment, Gertie took a deep breath and recovered.

"He needs human blood," Jeno said as Hector laid Klaus down on the couch. "He needs it now."

"He can have mine," Hector said.

Jeno shook his head. "Your blood is tainted with the virus."

"What about mine?" Phoebe offered.

"I can tell by your color that you don't have enough," Jeno said.

"Then mine," Mamá insisted. "Let him drink from me."

"Or me," Babá said. "You don't have to be the one, Marta."

"I have done this before," she said.

Babá's eyes grew wide. "What?"

"She can explain later," Jeno said. "We're running out of time."

Mamá extended her wrist, but Klaus only looked at her blankly.

"I can't," he said.

Gertie grabbed Mamá's arm and bit, taking a small sip for herself before pressing the wrist to Klaus's lips. "Please, Klaus."

Klaus was hesitant at first, but then he drank, and the pallor of his complexion diminished with each swallow.

A knock at the door startled them. Gertie could sense her mother on the other side of the door.

The others exchanged worried glances before Babá asked, "Who is it?"

"Diane," Gertie's mother called out. "Have I come at a bad time?"

"She can't see us like this!" Mamá whispered.

"Gertie is her daughter," Babá argued. "She has the right to know."

"Can you come in another hour?" Mamá asked with a strain in her voice as Klaus continued to drink.

"Of course," Diane said. "But is everything okay? You don't sound like yourself, Marta."

The doorknob turned, which, though imperceptible to human ears, was quite audible to Gertie. She dashed across the room to intervene.

As her mother pushed open the door to peer inside, Gertie crowded the narrow opening, even though the light from the stairwell burned.

"Gertie?" her mother asked. Her eyebrows lifted, disappearing behind her blonde bangs. "Oh, Gertie!"

"Please come back later," Gertie said as tears pricked her eyes. She hadn't expected to be overwhelmed with emotion at the sight of her mother. She told herself that it was the sunlight causing the tears, but she knew the truth. She hated this woman and loved her at the same time.

"I've been so worried," her mother said.

Gertie tried hard to hold her tongue before spitting out, "I doubt that."

"Gertoula!" Mamá called from inside. "Don't speak to your mother that way."

Gertie turned to Mamá. "She's not my mother." Her lips quivered as her throat tightened. She wanted to add, *You are.*

Diane turned even paler as she entered the room and closed the door behind her. When she noticed Klaus wiping the blood from his lips and Marta pressing a towel to her bleeding arm, her eyebrows disappeared behind her bangs again. "What's going on?"

"We were attacked," Hector said. "Turning Klaus was the only way to save him."

"I'm so sorry!" Diane said. "This is all my fault."

Gertie wrinkled her brow and asked, "How is this *your* fault? What have *you* got to do with any of this?"

"Oh," Diane placed her hand over her heart.

Gertie sensed she was having chest pains. "Mom?"

"I have so much to tell you, Gertie. I should have told you a long time ago. I'm so sorry."

"I'm listening," Gertie said. "Spit it out."

Gertie didn't wait for her mother to speak. She invaded her mind, seeking answers. Instead, she found confusion and muddled fragments. Seventeen years ago, a handsome man claiming to be a god, a warning, then a prophecy. Maybe if Gertie could lock eyes with her, she could see the past, like she did that time with Phoebe.

"Not now," Jeno said crossing the room to Gertie's side. "Look. I know you're anxious to understand your past, but we have to get Klaus to safety before nightfall."

"Why is Klaus in danger?" Nikita asked.

Mamá covered her face and slouched back in the sofa near Klaus's feet. "I can't take any more of this."

Gertie sensed that Mamá had been able to read Jeno's mind and had learned that Klaus would be controlled by Euripides.

But why hadn't Vladimir controlled Hector? Gertie blocked her mind as soon as the next thought entered: And why hadn't Jeno controlled *her*?

"You and Hector were less susceptible to the manipulation of your maker because you're demigods," Jeno said, as though he had heard *both* of her thoughts. "Phoebe was controlled by Vladimir, through Damien. That's why we couldn't communicate with her. He'd blocked her mind from us and ours from her. She had no choice but to follow his orders."

Phoebe's face turned red as Babá enfolded her in his arms.

"It's okay." Babá patted her head. "You couldn't help it."

"So why couldn't *you* control Damien?" Hector asked.

The mention of his name again brought more tears to Mamá's eyes. Her face went pale.

"I'm sorry," Hector muttered.

"I think my father brainwashed him," Jeno said. "Damien was too young…"

"Stop," Mamá pleaded. "Don't talk about it. I can't take it."

"I don't understand what's going on," Diane said. "Klaus is in trouble?"

"Yes," Jeno said. "The others will wait to attack again tonight, but Euripides can take control of Klaus's mind at any moment."

"So what do we do?" Babá asked.

"We need to restrain him," Jeno said. "And it would be best if we could take him some place far away from here."

"Come to New York," Diane said. "All of you."

Gertie's jaw dropped.

"We can't afford the flight…" Babá started to say.

"I can," Diane said. "I insist. This is my fault anyway. Give me the chance to help."

Gertie still didn't understand why her mother kept saying everything was her fault. She also did not like the idea of leaving Athens. The thought of the Angelis family seeing the luxury of her home compared to their own made her uncomfortable, too.

"What would Dad say?" she asked.

"He doesn't have to know," Diane replied. "He's in Venice. We found a house there."

Gertie searched Jeno's mind to get a sense for his opinion about his mother's suggestion. He wanted them all to go—without him.

"If you stay, so do I," Gertie said to him. She hadn't meant to say it out loud.

"No," Diane said. "If you want to know anything about your past, you have to come, too, Gertie."

"I'll stay here with Jeno," Hector offered. "Maybe we can convince Euripides…"

"If you two are staying, then…" Gertie began.

"No," Jeno interrupted. "Isn't it your duty to protect the Angelis family?" he said to Hector. "Euripides might get to Klaus even as far as New York. The first thing he'll do is make Klaus turn, or kill, his family. You have to be there to prevent that."

Nikita gasped.

"Jeno, you can't stay," Gertie said. "I won't know how to feed in New York."

As Gertie sensed the reproach among the humans, her face turned red. "I can't help it. I have no choice."

She wanted to scream, but she held back. Too many emotions were already filling the room. Her rage didn't need to be added into the mix. "And Klaus will need it, too. How will I do that, Jeno? How will I feed Klaus?"

"Please, Jeno." Marta crossed the room and took Jeno's hand. "Will you do it for me? I'm so frightened for Klaus. We need your help."

Babá frowned.

"I'll help you get settled," Jeno said. "But then I must return to my city." He turned to Hector. "You heard what Euripides said. He plans to make more vampires."

"We need to warn the other demigods." Hector took out his phone. "I'll hold a meeting, come up with a plan."

"Let them handle that," Jeno said. "You go to New York."

"They don't understand," Hector said. "They don't know what I know about your race."

Jeno read Hector's mind. "They despise us. You're worried they will try to exterminate us."

"Exactly," Hector said.

"How soon can you meet?" Gertie asked.

Hector rubbed his chin. "I bet I can get everyone together within the hour."

"We need to bind Klaus with something strong," Jeno said. "The iron chains from the basement."

Klaus's eyes widened. "You want to put me in that coffin?"

"Thee moy. I can't take this!" Mamá cried.

"It would be best if he traveled to New York in it," Jeno said. "It would be safer for him and for us."

Diane took out her phone. "What time should we fly out?"

"How soon can you be ready?" Jeno asked Marta.

EVA POHLER

Eva Pohler is a *USA Today* bestselling author of over thirty novels in multiple genres, including mysteries, thrillers, and young adult paranormal romance based on Greek mythology. Her books have been described as "addictive" and "sure to thrill"—*Kirkus Reviews*.

To learn more about Eva and her books, and to sign up to hear about new releases, and sales, please visit her website at www.evapohler.com.